David Ratcliffe lives in Glossop, Derbyshire having had various jobs ranging from Police Constable to Bus Driver. He has had short stories/articles widely published in the UK.

PRISONERS of LIMBO

DAVID RATCLIFFE

First published in Great Britain in 1997 by
Tanjen Ltd

ISBN 1 901530 04 3

Printed and bound in Great Britain by
Redwood Books, Trowbridge, Wiltshire

British Library Cataloguing in Publication Data.
A catalogue record for this book is available
from the British Library.

Tanjen Ltd
52 Denman Lane
Huncote
Leicester
LE9 3BS

to my wife Winifred for putting up with me ...

ONE

'WHY are you crying, Mary?'

It had been one of those great days you think back to when you're down. First, Tommy went with Dad to pick up the self-drive. Then they carried all the furniture out in the sun. Funny how you could stick all the junk you lived with all day into a box van.

Now Mum had to wreck it all by crying. There she was, sitting across from Dad in the lurching van, dark head bowed, leaking silent tears.

Dad didn't think a lot of it either, judging by his voice.

She'd nearly thrown a wobbler just looking round the bare walls of their old house. Sense or what? They were only swapping one council dump for another anyway. They'd still be treated like subculture even though New Casterleck was out in the country-side, an estate as brand spanking as its name.

Just to pile it on, now that the tears had come, so had the fog.

A hanging grey mist waited for them as they turned out of the A road traffic — a cloying curtain of ten thousand particles to the cubic centimetre.

'Sure this is it, Dad?'

'Yes. So shut it.'

Mist? It had this trick of straining the colour out of everything. Dad was forced to peer through the windscreen of the van. Okay, fair enough. But then he dropped to a low, groaning gear.

Boring.

Rick wouldn't have slowed by as much as a single K.

Tommy winced as though in pain at the thought of Rick. Rick had been his hero. What fourteen-year-old boy could have resisted his customised, black Ford Capri with its alloy wheels? And there was his catch phrase whispering from beneath the mop of black, greasy hair.

When you ride with Rick, you leave your earthly cares behind.

Rick had been dead six months, his beloved Capri a tangled mess of metal . . .

Wouldn't happen this trip. This was a Transit box van, and Dad wasn't Rick.

Tommy and Lucille were jammed glumly between Mum and Dad in the cab. Mum'd be thinking that Tommy and Dad wouldn't understand that moving house was an emotional thing for a woman. No Women's Lib for Mrs Mary Carter.

Lucy looked dead cheesed as well, lip curling beneath the flowing brown curls, resigned head on one side in one of her insolent, mickey taking, glassy stares.

Dad tried to lighten things up. He flashed Mum the grin he used on crumpet in the street when he was driving buses. He'd

8

think Tommy and Lucille were too young to suss it. Huh. Dream on.

That was when the light exploded.

It wasn't a sudden thing. A light, spangled curtain of air started drawing across the road ahead — shimmering air, flecked with yellow and gold.

Weird.

Already, it blocked their side of the carriageway, but Dad could have swerved round it. Instead, he just ploughed through. Maybe he was boringly right. It was only air and light after all. It was now too blinding to discern detail — just this heavy curtain of light. There was a roaring sound, too, like an aero engine . . .

Tommy was awed by the sensation of frozen helplessness; of being confronted by a natural force yet to be checked out by science, all-knowing in its conceit.

Wild!

The high was what grabbed Tommy — the pumping adrenalin high that drove the heart rate up and up. It was like being with Rick. Fear was excitement, and excitement was fear. Yeah!

'Jesus!'

'Don't take the Lord's name in vain, Thomas.'

'Aw, Mum! No-one believes in that stuff anymore!'

This meant he got chewed up by Dad. 'Have some respect for your mother, Tommy!'

OK, Frank didn't appreciate being distracted right then, grappling with steering, brakes, gears.

'Why don't I just top myself, yeah?'

. . . Funny. Did they all kinda doze off after the noise and light thing? Now they were pulling up on this mud road in front of these empty houses. Theirs was right on the front, opposite this silent mass of trees.

No-one came to look as they entered. Not a curtain stirred . . .

In the hall, in dull grey light, Tommy and Lucy listened to Mum sniffing into her hanky in the empty back room. Dad was droning words of comfort. Yeah, fair enough.

They gave each other that brother and sister look that meant — I Dare You. They slid out the door, away down the grey path, out onto the mud of the unmade road.

***

Tommy could have scripted what Mum and Dad were saying.

'Frank? Where're Thomas and Lucille?'

Frank would be unpacking two of the mugs for a brew. First thing's first, yeah? 'Out exploring, I reckon.'

'I hope they find their way back before dark.'

'They won't if you don't call them Tommy and Lucy like everybody else, Mary.'

'I call my children by the names they were baptised with in church, Francis . . .'

By now she'd be hanging up the picture of Pope John Paul — nothing more certain — and the one of her deceased father, taken with his WW2 air crew . . .

Giggling, Tommy and Lucy ran into the part built estate, leaving behind the boring pantomime of carrying in all the furniture. Lucy always made a big production out of laughing. Her jaw just hung right open revealing those front teeth with the animal split in the middle.

'What we gonna do, Tommy?'

'Explore!'

'Huh. Child . . .'

Tommy Carter slouched, head down, hands in pockets. He was a picture of teenage defiance. His brown hair was cut spiky, he wanted everyone to know he was trouble. His size meant no-one messed with him at school — when he was forced to show up that was. Lucy? She thought she was it, just 'cos she'd left school.

Huh.

Their trainers crunched on the dry earth and cinders of the unsurfaced roads and paths. Some of the houses were just shells, their glassless windows yawning like skull sockets in the slowly clearing grey of the mist.

No kids, no people, no movement.

Creepy.

They wandered back to the ring road. Its mud was deeply rutted by tracked, and big tyred, construction vehicles. Tommy could see a strange, square tower — a rising grey smudge poking above the roofs. It had to be somewhere in the centre of the estate. Because light and colour was still robbed from everything by the dull overcast, the structure looked insubstantial, as if it couldn't decide whether it was real or a mirage. It had a balcony with a handrail. Just a boring flat brick and concrete thing.

Tommy caught movement.

A man in a leather jacket had just walked up to the rail on the tower balcony and was leaning on it. Was he looking at Tommy and Lucy? Impossible to tell at this distance in such colourless murk.

Tommy shot a glance at Lucy. She'd switched on that speculative smile of hers like a light — the one where her bottom lip slid coyly behind the gapped front teeth. Huh.

Wordlessly, brother and sister crunched between the house units to investigate.

The guy at the rail just watched, growing more distinct as they approached. He wore a white scarf, limp in the lifeless air . . .

In the middle of the estate was an empty stretch of fenced earth edged by a cinder path and overgrown grass. There was a sign: SITE FOR PROPOSED NEW CASTERLECK COMMUNITY SCHOOL.

Tommy and Lucy slipped through a gap in the mesh fence. No sign of any proper buildings yet, just a wide expanse of tarmac that began and ended nowhere, like a piece cut out of an old black and white photo. The future school playground? No. The tarmac had been laid for yonks. Grass and weeds grew out of wound-like splits caused by decades of bitter frosts.

Of the square tower or the guy in the beat up flying jacket there was no sign.

'Hey!'

A burly figure in orange cagoule, site boots and white hardhat was standing a few metres away. He'd just appeared. His face was indeterminate, hidden in the drab grey shade of the hat. His voice was husky — a throaty whisper.

'This is a bad place.'

Lucy shrieked: her usual theatrical mixture of fear and delight. She fled for the fence, arms poised in her girlish way. Great!

Tommy thrust his hands defiantly in his pockets, even though he knew that a white hat meant Boss. 'There's no sign, Mister. I go where I want, right?'

Again, the guttural whisper. 'Wrong.'

A work callused hand swished through the air and went smack against Tommy's cheek. Before the sullen boy could recover, the hand grabbed his collar. Cheek stinging, he was frog-marched toward the gap in the fence.

'You can't do that, Mister!'

There was only the quiet croak. 'I can. I have.'

The rough hand pitched Tommy through the fence. He scraped his knees in the process. Rubbing them in petulant fury, he glared at the bulk of the retreating orange back.

The white hat bobbed in the grey gloom.

***

In the dull light of the kitchen, Frank and Mary lingered over the coffee mugs. Mary watched Frank light a candle, chuckling to himself. The wan flame would make her eyes look moist. His grin of expectancy saddened her. He would hurry her.

'Let's just sit for a minute, Frank. This could be a fresh start. A change of luck.'

'Ye-es . . .'

His voice was lascivious, both eyes pinpointed by the candle flame. He was acting the villain in a children's pantomime. Mary knew he was trying to make her smile. He always did things the same way. He even used the same mock US accent she'd listened to for seventeen years when he was in this frame of mind.

'Tell me ya love me.'

As she allowed herself, dutifully, to be pulled onto his lap, Mary could not prevent her gaze from drifting. There was so much unpacking to do. At least the picture of Pope John Paul was on the wall, right there, next to the icon of the Sacred Heart and Dad's silver framed, wartime crew photo.

Worryingly, she caught herself daydreaming as Frank's hands slid comfortingly over her hips. She was imagining they belonged to someone else — a dark, exciting spirit . . .

This was enough to make her freeze with guilt. Mary shut her eyes tight before she could see Frank's smile fade like the Cheshire Cat in reverse.

Odd.

She could smell earth. Damp. Cold. Her left side felt it was exposed to a draught. The hand became rough, callused — truly, like someone else's. Soon, her lips parted with pleasure in the flickering candlelight.

'Oh!'

***

'Lucy!'

Tommy's plaintive cry just bounced back at him from the shells of the half completed housing units. Shrugging, he gave up looking for his sister and returned to the central site, taking care to keep hidden.

From the prefabricated shell of a windowless unit, Tommy watched White Hat disappear up wooden steps into a raised site cabin. Teeth gritted with hate, Tommy scuttled through the near twilight.

He wriggled under the fence, marine-crawled across the dried mud and squirmed beneath the site cabin — a mobile propped on brick piles. Above his brown, spiky head he could hear the drone of men's voices.

At the foot of the wooden steps was a bag of tools.

***

Lucy gasped, giggling fit to bust. She stopped running when she reached the cinder path.

Gapped teeth showing beneath the brown curls, she teetered on tiptoe trying to see over the wild briars and dog grass — but she was unable, even when she jumped, lycra tights bending and straightening, athletic above the Madonna boots.

Cheeks glowing, she paused, smile fading.

Footsteps.

Someone was striding along the cinder path, just out of sight around the long curve. Strong, male strides.

Lucy straightened her tumbling curls, smile reappearing, bottom lip hiding. Had to be male. A yellow spot weaved above the briars. One of the construction gang. Lean. Young. As he strode, his head was lowered beneath the issue hardhat which cast his face into obscure and tantalising shadow.

Funny. No eyes glinted beneath the brim of the hardhat. The young man just kept coming, obviously unaware of Lucy's tingling presence, tool bag on his shoulder — would have passed on by in the grey light.

'Hi . . .'

The site boots slowed, came to a halt on the black cinders. The pale yellow of the hat brim remained low.

Smiling, Lucy thrust herself against her patterned jersey. OK, the toilet paper she'd lined her bra with felt soggy. It had been there all day. Lucy advanced toward the young male; advanced with coy little steps.

'Do ya know the way to the ring road?'

Inching forward.

The figure stayed gaunt in the grey, like a robot with the power cut, face a shadowy smudge of charcoal. The powerful shoulders began to swing slightly.

Lucy hid behind red fingertips. She loved that male strut and swagger that showed pride in being noticed. Her cheeks burned. Her nipples tingled within the soggily padded out bra.

She sidled right up to the stark, proud figure in the pale yellow hardhat; close enough to take a palpitating peek under the brim.

Lucy's jaw fell open, mouth forming a cartoon O.

Her eyes showed white all round the irises.

A work hardened palm settled on her cringing shoulder making her flinch and squeal at the figure. 'What's up with ya face?'

A guttural whisper emerged from the throat, as if there was no mouth.

'*You like?*'

The hand that gripped the patterned jersey was hard. Not cold, but . . . It felt like it was made of the scaffolding and rough timber it handled all day.

'No!'

Lucy was being dragged through an unmade garden space into an unfinished unit. The unnatural grip almost lifted her clean off her feet.

'No need for this caveman stuff!'

The stride was unchecked, like that of a pre-programmed automaton. The hard hand pushed her inside the unit, slamming her, pinning her, to the breeze block end wall.

Mortar dust hung between them. A cloud. Lucy felt its particles settle on her cheek. It was shadowy in here, but not natural —

just a lack of light. The face that loomed over her below the pale grey of the hardhat was just a darker lack of light. Feeble.

The voice, like the hand, remained inhuman.

'*I w a n t y o u r—*'

'I . . . I want, too.' Lucy tried to take the fearful stare out of her gaze, mouth working nervously.

'*G i v e.*'

'Yes. All right. I'll give. I like fellas, yeah? Weakness . . . Always getting shit 'cos of it. Let go. Yeah? I won't run. OK?'

Slowly, unable to take her eyes off the charcoal figure standing motionless before her, Lucy lifted the hem of her jersey. Lifted it over her head. Let it flop to the dirt. Smiled.

'You a robot or what? Put the tool bag down at least!'

The tools clinked as the bag fell. Lucy coiled the white bra on top of it. Her hand, as uncertain as a butterfly, reached across the dusty space between them, took the hardhat, placed it on her own head.

She smiled, jerkily, quivering. 'You're not real.'

His hands began to claw at her tights.

'OK. OK. You gonna explode or what?'

Lucy barely had time to remove her knickers before he was on top of her. She almost felt ridiculous, her knickers balanced precariously on one foot, stale breath misting her face. He was cold inside her.

There was a guttural sigh . . .

When the charcoal shape had done what it wanted, it bent, tossed aside the bra, picked up the tool bag and left.

Wriggling into her lycra tights, Lucy, breathless (and thrilled), shouted after the striding figure.

'Screw you!'

Without breaking its stride, the figure in the yellow hardhat entered the site, marched to the raised cabin, dumped its tool bag at the foot of the wooden steps, and opened the door.

***

Beneath the site cabin, Tommy Carter's dark eyes glinted. He thought about slipping away with the entire tool bag.

But he'd be seen from the window. Fat old workmen in cagoules would pour out like hippos, shouting obscenities at him as he fled through the gathering murk towards the fence he shouldn't have entered.

A giggle burst from him — a high of blood pumping adrenalin.

Too risky. Don't get mad — get even . . .

Flinching, he heard the roar of an approaching engine. He could see the turning, ribbed tyres of an advancing truck. With much crashing of gears, it reversed up to the steps. Tommy could see the throbbing prop shaft rotating, feel and hear the vibrating transmission. A cable tightened on the grey underside of the truck as it shuddered to stillness. Boots and wellingtons thudded up the steps.

Overhead, the tone of the rough, male voices heightened distinctly.

'Hi, Keith — Mr Foreman!'

Tommy studied the underneath of the truck, piggy eyes moving slyly in his head. There was the earth covered back axle and differential, fuel and brake pipes. His grubby hand slid like a snake into the tool bag.

It emerged with a stout pair of side cutters.

Moments later, his teeth gleamed with delight. A pool of brake fluid was forming close to one of the deeply patterned tyres.

Tommy sighed. His eyes shone in the dark grey beneath the hut. Blood and adrenalin rushed through his veins and arteries. And there was that funny feeling in his loins that he didn't quite understand — only that it meant buzz. What did they call it? A cheap thrill.

His knees didn't hurt quite so bad now.

As he prepared to slither away, a white Range Rover cruised quietly to a halt a few metres from the truck. From it climbed another guy in a white hardhat. Green wellingtons stomped through the dirt — but this boss wore a suit.

He clumped up the wooden steps.

Distinctly, a voice said, 'Mr Ryland?'

By then, Tommy had writhed halfway across the dried mud of the site to the fence.

***

Tommy met with Lucy on the corner near the house. She grinned that gap-toothed grin of hers and she looked as bedraggled as he did. Huh. Surprise!

'Met a farmer's boy, yeah, Lucy?'

'Shut it!'

'S'all right. Each to their own poison.'

'Just keep ya nose out, right?'

'Yeah, right, sure, Luce.'

She didn't snarl at Dad when he flung the door open. 'Thought you two head bangers had got lost, you fools!'

'Sorry, Dad,' said Tommy before the disbelieving gaze. 'Had a struggle finding the right row, yeah?'

'Digging a tunnel were you?' Frank pointed at the mud on their jeans and tops. 'Get sandblasted and washed. You can have your tea, even though you've panicked your mum.'

At the table, Mum and Dad exchanged soppy looks. Tommy scoffed silently, clattering his knife and fork. 'Which is my room?'

Frank placed his utensils neatly together as Mum looked. 'You, my son, are having the box room at the front. Lovely view of the woods!'

'Huh. Might've known —'

'Watch your mouth, lad. We're having the master bedroom. There're two of us, and we are the masters. Lucy's having the other because she's a big girl and will soon be working — or better had be soon. It's fair . . .'

Up in the tiny box room, Tommy found that Mum had hung the curtains. Funny how such things gave the brain-dead-old pleasure. Tommy leaned on the emulsioned sill and luxuriated in the new house smell. He scored a thin groove in the new paint with his penknife.

He stared with his dark eyes at the night sky and thought about his old mate, Rick . . .

Six months ago, Rick cruised up beside him on the street in his hand-rollered black Ford Capri.

'Ride with Rick, man.'

Great! Being pressed back into the seat by the power acceleration brought The Buzz every time. Cheap thrills abounded. Tommy loved everything about the experience of riding with Rick. Excitement with style. The guy was so laid back, yeah? In his twenties, Rick was considered a fool, wasting his life riding around showing off. They just didn't understand.

Simply watching his cool manner in that driving seat said it all — the black hair, greased till it shone, black leathers, jewellery. On Rick's right hand, third finger, was a dull pewter ring in the shape of a skull. OK, such gear was out of time, but Rick could carry it off.

In no time they were in the country. It had just been raining and you could see steam rising in the sun. Rick slid into this bend. Slid. Not a skid. Not intentional.

'Slow down, Rick. We're losing it!'

'Rick loses nothing, man.'

Shadow. It just grew on the opposite hedgerow. Something big was coming round the bend, its shadow cast by the low sun.

'We'll be killed, Rick!'

'Rick cannot be killed, man.'

For the first time, Tommy was so frightened he was no longer in tune with Rick. The Buzz was there, the usual electric surge, but now polluted with fear, the sudden realisation he was mortal, that he may not survive. He wanted to survive, was almost shocked by his desperate need to continue to breathe.

Especially when the thirty-four ton juggernaut kinda trundled round the bend. The driver's face was an angry blur. Rick was cutting the bend as he always did.

Air brakes hissed.

Big tyres locked.

The big tank of the articulated trailer started to jack-knife round till it covered the entire width of the steaming road. It even blocked the sun. Rick jerked the wheel a little. The black Capri was now sideways on to its destiny and travelling quite slowly.

Chrome buckles jingled as Tommy shed the safety belt. He always remembered Rick's last words.

'Earthly cares, man. Earthly cares . . .'

Well, hell! Tommy did care — cared about Life. His life. So he threw open the front passenger door. Baled out. Deserted Rick at the Moment of Truth. Safely, he rolled into the hedgerow. Saw the impact.

The sliding, unstoppable articulated tank swept straight over the black Capri like a giant guillotine. It neatly decapitated everything above the long sleek bonnet of the Capri, structure and contents.

The bottom half of the Capri rolled right on.

Headless . . .

***

From his box room window, Tommy saw that the stars were still visible above the mist that shrouded the trees.

Weird.

The stars didn't twinkle. As he watched, one or two disappeared. He began to hear the same roar he'd heard in the self-drive van when the strange light had appeared. This time, he could identify it more clearly.

Aero engines. Firing badly.

Tommy blinked to clear his vision as he folded the penknife and replaced it in his jeans. An old, piston engined aircraft was approaching out of the night. One wing was raised. It was so low, it was heading straight for him.

Four engines.

One of the propellers was still. Smoke poured. Streaming flame licked the wing root. The nose of the aircraft was perspex. Tommy could see it glint in the pale light of the hidden moon.

He ducked below the now scarred windowsill.

'Dear Jesus!'

He prayed like Mum had made him as a kid.

'If I should die before I wake, I pray the Lord my soul to take . . .'

The roar of the badly synchronised engines was actually rattling the glass. His models and CDs that Mum had carefully laid out for him danced and travelled on the shelf Dad had already put up.

Like the blink of a monster eye, a shadow blotted out the pale square of window cast by the moon on the opposite wall.

The roar cut off . . .

Tommy's face screwed up like it did when he was pretending to be asleep before Dad's sceptical gaze. Tiny creaking sounds escaped from the back of his tensing throat. His legs drew up beneath him as his bowels tightened as he waited for the rending crash and the inevitable blast of superheated magnesium. His cringing mind's eye flashed him glimpses of terror filled, helmeted faces and raised arms and gauntlets behind the perspex.

Last, unholy seconds clicked by . . .

Tommy screwed up into the tight little ball of the foetal position; he opened one eye in the oppressive silence. The single, exposed iris checked every corner of the room. Everything was intact. One of his models was half hanging off the shelf. The square window of moonlight flickered slightly on the wall.

Shaking, Tommy raised his head above the sill.

The trees stood guard in their wispy cloaks. A plume of oily smoke was dissipating in the dead sky. The drifting smoke spread, thinned, dispersed.

As if it had never been.

The stars hung undisturbed above the black profile of the wood. They might have been daubed and dabbed by a celestial child. Not a leaf twitched in the mist as the last tendrils of smoke were spirited away like expended, temporary life.

With dread anticipation, Tommy opened his other eye.

Noise. Another roar. A normal, truck engine.

Craning his neck, Tommy could see the truck from the building site. It was just rounding the bend in the ring road. It was an open back job with a plastic moulded site cabin lashed on. Tommy felt he caught glimpses of more frightened faces stark above huddled cagoules and donkey jackets. As Tommy watched, the truck wobbled. The engine screamed.

The truck left the road.

It bumped and swayed dangerously over the mud until it toppled

There was an inevitability about the forward motion of the sliding truck. Keeling over on its side or not, it was unstoppable — like the tanker; like the aircraft. Finally, it did spill gracefully onto its side. But the forward motion was maintained.

It crashed into the trees.

Tommy could hear the crash, the impact; almost feel the splinter and crack of the decimated trunks, the shredding of branches and bark.

But the trees remained sentinel.

Tommy blinked.

The trees merely closed ranks as the screech of metal continued in the wood. There was no bang, no fire, no smoke. Just trees, standing like guardsmen with blank faces, unable or unwilling to divulge a damn thing . . .

For endless seconds, Tommy remained at the sill gaping at the stolid mass of the dark wood. He opened the window. The night air chilled his face as he peered out.

He noted the drainpipe snaking down past the porch roof like a fireman's pole . . .

***

Frank got the portable TV going, but there was only blank snow on the screen.

He gave a growl of impatience that made Mary flinch as she unfolded his bus jacket. His bus shirt hung on the door like a ghost.

'Looks like the aerial got broke in transit,' said Frank. 'I'll pick another one up when I take the van back tomorrow between my split duty.'

The snow shrank to a dot amid the dark grey. Frank disconnected the terminals from the old car battery. Mary sensed him mooching around as she fastened the suitcase and bustled it away. She lit a candle in front of the icon, clasped her hands in prayer.

When she'd finished, Frank slumped on the couch. 'Luck . . .' he said.

Mary brought the lit candles from the dining table to the coffee table.

'You're always doing something,' he said. 'Sit down.'

She did. At the far end of the couch. When he turned to her, reaching for her, she said, 'These candles are depressing. When are they going to switch the electric on?'

Releasing air from his lungs, Frank lifted his raw boned frame from the couch. He expelled air like steam.

'It'll soon be morning,' he sighed.

***

Tommy landed on the mud without a sound. Mum and Dad were asleep. Even Lucy. He'd waited so long he felt he could see brush-strokes of lighter grey in the east.

He crossed the unmade ring road and found that after a few short metres of the trees, the mud gave way to grass. A sharp change. As though it were part of another countryside altogether.

Tommy examined the bark of the trees. There was no scarring, no gouges in the grass where he'd seen the truck go in.

A shape flew out of the silence of the wood.

The boy cowered in sudden terror, throwing up his arms the way he'd seen the aviators do in the burning aircraft.

It was a barn owl.

Tommy laughed: a playground bully caught, then let off. His vocal release of tension was soaked up by the massed trees without echo.

His laugh died when he heard the footfalls.

Heavy boots crashed against the grass and earth. Stalks and wild blooms were crushed beneath the encroaching tread. In the gloom, Tommy saw movement.

A bobbing white shape.

Fused to the forest floor, Tommy watched the pale hardhat draw nearer. The dull orange of the cagoule materialised from the deepest of greys as the construction boss approached.

'You!'

OK, it was just possible that Tommy had dozed off at the windowsill and dreamed of fantasy air and truck crashes — maybe through mourning Rick. But this was cast iron real. Sight, sound — the works.

An arm grew out of the dirty orange-grey of the cagoule as the burly figure pointed directly at him, tearaway council house kid. The mouth of dread authority formed a darker grey in the looming, charcoal face.

'You fool!'

TWO

WHEN Frank Carter awoke, the first streaks of a lighter grey glimmered indistinctly in the east.

The alarm was not due to go off for another five minutes, so he depressed the clock lever. Mary snored gently beside him, the duvet tucked beneath her with that knack of the impenetrable she had. Frank gave her a long look, then got up.

As he dressed in the bathroom, he wondered what had woken him up so suddenly. Then he discovered that when he held his breath he could hear it.

Music.

Probably, it was a trucker or a postie getting ready for work, listening to the radio.

As Frank climbed into the self-drive, he saw movement above the trees. A bird of prey was plunging. An owl. Maybe a hawk. This was the country, he reminded himself contentedly. Mary would find it right up her street when she got used to it. She might even relax, mellow out.

Smiling drippily, Frank started the engine. Above the trees were wisps of smoke, darker than the mist, though clearing rapidly. Something had been burning in the woods. The hanging fog soon enveloped it.

As he drove away, horror tightened his fingers on the wheel. His stomach felt like his large intestine had fallen out.

The mist brought back a memory . . .

A new driver on the buses, he was doing a dead run back from dropping his passengers at his last destination after midnight. The conductor was cashing up on the back seat. They were flying along a country road rather like this one: sweeping curves shrouded in trees and fog. Something was lying in the road. Something striped.

Frank eyeballed it as a discarded mattress.

Only when he was right on top of it did he discern arms and legs. A head. The tyres shrieked in the darkness. The back end of the decker swung half round in a skid.

The conductor, an old sweat called Reg, came shambling down the aisle like a wounded bear, black hair hanging over his eyes.

'What's up, matey?'

Moments later, they were looking down at the mangled body in the road. It was once a young, blonde woman, beautiful, in a striped mini dress. Reg bent down to her, gasping and wheezing with a dedicated lack of fitness.

'Dead as a doornail,' he pronounced.

Frank stared. Perhaps he was hoping that a hard blink and a shake of the head would dispel the stark image. 'It's shit time for me,' he said.

Reg rasped his blue jowls. 'Are you dead certain you hit her? I felt nowt.'

Frank tried it. He blinked. Hard. The body in the striped dress did not go away. 'I know the front wheels missed. She was lying in the road right here, where she is now.'

Reg grasped him round the shoulders. 'Then it's got nowt to do with us, has it?'

'We can't just leave her there, Reg!'

'She's dead, matey.' Reg went on clasping his shoulders, letting him ruminate over her; letting him note that she had no face, just a bloodied mess of congealed gore, individuality and identity ripped away by some speed freak.

'You gonna give her the kiss of life, matey?'

'Jesus, Reg!'

'She's with Jesus right now, matey, filling in her forms at the pearly gates. If she assed about too much in yon mini dress, she'll be stoking Old Nick's boilers. Either way, it's nowt to do with us. We could give her a bloody state funeral, nothing would alter. Eh?'

Reg's eyes glinted beneath the staring moon as he went on.

'Who's gonna know if we piss off now, eh? Eh?'

'Reg! It's our duty!'

The blue jowls moved closer with their insidious whisper. 'If you'd caused the accident, the law you crap yourself so much over tells ya to sing like a shell shocked budgie. As it is, matey, what law says you got to do owt? Eh?'

Frank shook his head dumbly, unable to take his eyes off the graphic horror in the road. There seemed to be a magnetism, an energy, that bound the two of them. 'I thought it was a mattress, Reg.'

The whisper continued at his shoulder, just behind his left ear. 'It wasn't a frigging mattress, but you thought it was a mattress.

That's it, matey. You drove past it thinking it was a frigging mattress. I was cashing up and saw and felt and heard and thought nowt. Good guards never see nowt, matey. By the shortness o' that dress, I'd say she probably was a mattress.'

The sweaty palm tightened on Frank's left shoulder.

'Don't bugger yourself before you've even started in this job, lad. You've got a wife an' two babbies. Be the bloody Pharisee. Let's piss off . . .'

Frank drove the self-drive on through the mist and the trees, head bent as if expecting a blow. It was all so long ago. Meaningless . . .

When Frank had asked old stagers at his old depot about directions to Casterleck, they'd laughed.

'When the sheep are bowlegged fore and aft, you'll know you're there!'

Instead of sheep, he came across a cow.

It stood in the centre of an isolated crossroads. It was black. There was a bell around its neck.

There was no way around it so Frank had to pull up. It stared through the windscreen at him with a disturbing communication and intelligence. Even accusation. Frank flashed the van headlights. It stood motionless. Its bell just hung. Endless seconds passed, cold touching the back of Frank's neck.

Then it moved.

It shambled slowly to the side of the lane, bell dinging mournfully. The white of a rolling eye reflected the headlights in the gloom.

As Frank drove on, breathing hard, a cock crowed.

An old sign, black letters on white, proclaimed Old Casterleck to be half a mile away.

Houses began suddenly. Old stone cottages. They gave way to a long wall of crumbled brick and stone, a wrought iron gate. Then shops. A set of traffic lights, curiously futuristic, changed on his lone approach — as though he were expected. There was no movement down any of the side streets of terraced, stone dwellings. No glimmer of electric light speckled the shades of grey. On his left was the street he was looking for.

Mangle street . . .

The Old Casterleck Bus Depot was at the top of this short street. Its iron shutters were closed. Above them was a peeling sign: CHARON ROAD CAR CO LTD — just black stencilled lettering on faded white. Very old. The long, gabled building showed no lights. Its iron roof was dull in the washed out light. Two buses were parked on a square of concrete at the rear.

Frank parked the van in a corner and got out. His footsteps gritted flatly on the setts. Houses backed on to the old iron railings at the side of the compound. Elsewhere, fields rolled almost to infinity. In the far distance were the broad hulls of hills. Beyond the fence, a small river flowed lazily. A National Parks sign labelled it: RIVER LETHE.

A wicket door opened to one turn of its knurled brass knob. Inside, buses were jammed in four ranks. The nozzle of the fuel pump rested on a cut-down jerry can. There was the work smell of oil, diesel, dirt.

It was just possible to squeeze between the rows of vehicles to the shutters at the front. Beside these, Frank found a panel of light switches — the old round type. With much flickering, and hum of tired starter motors, strip lighting blinked into life.

Frank stared.

Several seconds passed before he could identify the cause of his feeling of what-is-wrong-with-this-picture?

He ran. Adrenalin-produced electricity jerked through his nervous system. He ran to the centre of the shutters, snapped up the cast iron locking bars with a grunt, pushed and pulled one of the heavy doors along its greased track, soles sliding and scrabbling in grease and dirt.

Out in Mangle Street, Frank took several deep breaths of heavy, grey air. Fearfully, he peeped back into the depot.

The figure was still there.

It was standing quietly next to the bus parked up front outside the Inspector's office.

It was a bus conductor.

He was wearing a peaked cap and the old style blue serge uniform of a past era.

Hanging on a strap of work shiny leather was an Ultimate ticket machine, as used in the 1950s.

***

The pointing finger projecting from the orange cagoule turned into a callused claw as Tommy gawked. It gripped him by the collar.

'Come. See what you have done.'

White Hat just strode right on through the wood. Tommy's feet barely touched the ground. No amount of desperate struggling or kicking could release him from the inhuman grasp as the construction boss marched deeper into the forest.

The white hardhat bobbed, the face beneath the brim an indeterminate grey in the mist that had to force apart to let them through. The drab light was paling as the moon was replaced by the rise of the tip of the watery sun.

Tommy gazed up at the charcoal smudge of the uncompromising features. The site boots went on crushing the greenery. The unforgiving face floated below the hardhat like dry parchment that had been stored for decades.

Until reawakened . . .

***

Mary was in bed. She was cold. A growing pallid light from the window revealed why.

She was alone.

Frank must have already left to begin the early part of his split — his first day at Casterleck Depot. Bleary eyed, Mary looked out of the window. Pity it was another dull, cheerless day.

Ten tenths, Mary . . .

This was what Father used to say on such days. He'd used old RAF terms till the day he died. Perhaps the War had been ingrained in his psyche. The photograph of him with his old crew was in its silver frame that winked near the picture of Pope John Paul downstairs. Mary sighed. She still didn't know why he'd waited more than a decade after the war to start a family. Asking him had brought only evasion and awkward changes of subject.

Outside, tendrils of mist hung near the woods. No footfall disturbed the still grey. Not surprising. The house was the only completed unit on the row — and the electricity was still not connected.

The box room was empty too. Mary shivered, the window had been left open, but the curtains remained deathly still. Closing the window, she wondered if Tommy saw freedom out there, in this cold, grey place, or was it merely the opportunity for further mischief.

The boy would be back when he was hungry, as Frank had so often pointed out. But the worry still made her chew her nails pensively.

Downstairs, Mary found a disturbing detail. The chain was still on the front door. Frank must have let himself out at the back. He knew she had a terror of being alone in a house not properly secured. Tommy? He'd have sneaked out of the window. Boys! Mary undid the chain and bolt at the front; was actually looking in the bin alcove for the milk before cursing her stupidity. There'd been no time to arrange local delivery. She'd have to put on her coat and seek out the local shops.

Someone would be around, surely . . .

***

Tommy's jaw sagged when he saw the first corpse.

The striding White Hat was dragging him past a large, ribbed truck tyre. It was disembodied at the foot of a tree. The corpse was hanging from the bole of another tree. Its overall clad leg was twisted between the branch roots at an impossible angle.

Something white was sticking out of the blood ringed material. Bone.

***

Head scarf fluttering, Mary trudged along the unmade ring road.

There were deep scars on the mud and the grass strip near the tree line. She could just see them. Something to do with the ongoing construction work, no doubt. They made her step falter. Whatever had caused them had cut a deep swathe in the trees. Broken trunks glimmered pale in the mist.

Then Mary's head jerked back to the houses like a sparrow's. She could hear the clink of milk bottles. Her gaze, searching the crescent roads, was caught by a square building. It was distant and vague in the thinning murk — just a smear of deeper grey above the rooftops. Perhaps it marked where the shops must be in the middle of the estate.

Mary Carter continued to cut between the part built units, but kept an ear cocked for the tell-tale whine of an electric milk float.

Instead, she heard the clip-clop of hooves.

Eventually, she saw the cart between the house shells. It was being pulled by a large, pale cart horse. Quaint, but it figured. Mary realised the estate had actually been laid out in the middle of a large, rural plain.

The horse came to a halt. Condensation hung about its snorting nostrils. Its eye rolled round to look at the bent figure of the milkman himself.

The milkman wore gauntlets, which seemed odd. How could he handle the bottles? He worked in a leather jacket and a strange helmet with split-lensed goggles.

'Yoo hoo!'

Mary bustled toward him, but the man remained bent over his crates. The crates were of the old type — galvanised metal. The bottles were quaint too. Had to be local farm milk with those wide necks — straight from the cow. Mm.

Mary scurried closer, smiling expectantly and politely, purse already in hand.

The helmeted head turned.

Mary stopped hurrying. Slowed to a stop. Stared.

The face beneath the helmet — it was horribly disfigured, worse than anything in any video nasty she'd caught Tommy with. A great purple burn distorted a swollen cheek and eye. Half the jaw was exposed, devoid of flesh so that he sported a constant, half grinning rictus of the rotted dead.

The voice croaked like a demon's.

'*Why are you here?*'

***

Matt Ryland drove his Company Range Rover once more up to the New Casterleck site cabin. Clamping a fresh cheroot between his white teeth, he flung himself from the vehicle.

With increasing apoplexy, he glared at the surrounding mud, the uncleared tarmac, the vast number of incomplete units. His sight the previous day of the boy slithering from beneath the hut was now only a minor irritation in his memory banks. Angrily, he clumped up the wooden steps and let the hut door crash open against the stop. It vibrated like a living organism.

Cowed faces gaped sullenly back at him from beneath yellow hardhats as they gathered round the stove drinking their damned tea from their damned chipped mugs.

'Keith Doyle!' he roared. 'He who calls himself a foreman. Come out, come out, wherever you are!'

The construction gang shuffled apart like the Red Sea to reveal the site foreman slumped in front of the wall plan. He turned his burly figure full on and scratched his cropped head. 'Good morning, Mr Ryland, sir.'

Clipboard in hand, Matt Ryland barged through the retreating gang and stabbed a finger at the wall plan.

'This is where you're supposed to be, building-wise. This is where you actually are . . .' The white fingers indicated two lines where colour codes ended and began. 'OK. Maybe there's something wrong with my eyesight, but don't you find there's a slight discrepancy?'

Ryland threw the clipboard onto the desk in front of the weary giant of a foreman they all knew, and once loved, as Keith Doyle.

Keith picked up the clipboard and inspected it, sucking his teeth in silent fury.

'Those sheets,' growled Ryland, 'show lines of figures.'

'Yeah, I know, Matt.'

'Don't even think about "Matt-ing" me when you're eye deep in the brown stuff, Doyle! Those figures show a) penalty clauses exacted, and b) bonuses —'

Here, he faced the gang of labourers and tradesmen to re-emphasise the word.

'*Bonuses* deducted!'

As Keith looked up, Ryland glared at them all. They lowered their heads. 'And before you start bellyaching, I can inform you guys that I get bonuses too. And because you've been dragging your butts, my bonus has also been deducted. So my sympathy is nil!'

Politely, Keith Doyle handed the clipboard back to Ryland.

Ryland snatched it in ritual rage, held it against his business suit, bellowed his final word.

'Talk!'

Boots and wellies shifted on the mud covered boards. Throats were cleared. Heads were scratched.

Keith cut through the general fidgeting with his calm Northern tones. 'We've thrown up all kinds of constructions in all kinds of conditions, Mr Ryland — gales on the east coast, storms in Scotland, floods in the west. Not once has this gang evoked penalties . . .'

Murmurs of agreement grew until Keith waved them down.

'I know resting on laurels is no attitude, but I've never seen such a catalogue of disasters and conditions in twenty-five years — and neither have you, Mr Ryland, if you care to check it out.'

It was Ryland's turn to cut through the Greek chorus. 'What do you mean by "conditions"?'

Keith waved one of his huge hands, criss-crossed with scars, a testimony to the number of hours it had spent on building sites. 'The first accident was on the first night. The crane came down — despite the extra ballast weight I ordered.'

Ryland drummed his white fingers on the desk. 'Conditions, Keith. Accidents ain't conditions.'

Keith's heavy face remained calm. 'The conditions cause the accidents.'

'Go on.'

'That first night, a freak wind blew all the prefabricated gables down like a row of dominoes. No. Dominoes are neat. These flats looked like a giant kid had stomped all over them — for fun!'

Yellow hardhats nodded and there were growls of confirmation.

Ryland grinned in triumph. 'I guessed you'd come up with the one about the weather, so I requested a report from the Met office. It's right here.' He turned up a sheet of paper on his board. 'I quote: "Between the dates indicated, no unusual weather has been reported in this entire region."'

As laughter rang, Keith glared in stoic menace. 'We were here, Mr Ryland. We saw the crane topple in the wind that wasn't reported by people who weren't here. I took the driver to hospital myself. Perhaps you'd care to phone his wife and discuss your Met report.'

Ryland relit his cheroot. 'You know and I know we can't make inclement weather claims on the contract unless the Met office confirms it.' He stalked to the door. 'I'm now going to inspect the site myself — unaccompanied. I'll soon know if my wire's being pulled. Delegate your tasks, Popeye, but remain here until my return.'

Ryland left behind an uneasy silence. Using Doyle's nickname, normally reserved for drunken, informal occasions, in front of the men in such a manner was calculated to humiliate. Now Doyle had to recover his authority.

'Guess I'll be needing that spinach,' he remarked dryly.

They was an almost tangible sense of relief and the men laughed.

'Now listen,' Doyle started and the laughter immediately stopped. They'd seen that look before. 'We're up to our necks in shit. And now we've got to crawl out of it.'

They gathered round him like children without a brain between them. Doyle had done his time, and the men respected him for that, though they would never admit it to his face.

'We're doing our best,' one of them piped up. 'It's these wankers in suits coming in with an 'ology and screwing up the job.'

Keith Doyle shook his head, slab face reddening. 'Ryland didn't foul up — we did. Take yesterday. Small thing. I found a kid trespassing on the site, bold as brass. You know what that'll lead to.'

'What did ya do, Boss?'

'Clipped his earhole.'

To Keith's weary annoyance, laughter crashed back, as if they thought everything was OK again. 'Ooh, you'll go straight to Hell for that one, Keith! The Court of Human Rights . . .' The rest was lost in an avalanche of more goddamn laughter.

Keith Doyle felt like banging his monolithic head on the desk. As the "desk" was only a trestle, he used his palm instead. 'You've got today's jobs! Do you like sex and travel?'

They gaped at him. 'Yeah . . .'

It was too easy.

'Then fuck off and get on with it then.'

There was an immediate exodus out of the hut.

Alone, he swung his bulk round to look at the wall plan. A funny feeling crept up his spine. Just an idea — that they were all as much a product of intended action, even imagination, as the goddamn wall chart. Could Thought, Energy, kid itself it was real?

A yellow hardhat peeked round the door as an afterthought. 'Reckon ya can save our jobs, Gaffer?'

A marker pen bounced uselessly off the hardhat.

'No!'

***

The yellow hardhat of the dead man lolled in the trees. The sightless eyes glared at Tommy in petrified accusation.

'Noo-oo!' screamed Tommy.

The callused hand of White Hat thrust him to within centimetres of the dead, hanging face.

The rest of the construction crew were half spilled out of the smashed plastic site cabin on the back of the truck. The truck itself was still lying on its side, entwined in the trunks of the trees that guarded it.

Funny.

One of the trunks was growing straight through the cab.

Its base began in one side window, and the trunk just grew straight up through the other side window — as if it had always been there.

'Please, God!'

Tommy brought his hands together, clasped them tightly. Faces were piled together like those of discarded, tailor's dummies. Each was frozen in its own silent scream of terror, of prayer. Hands clawed in plea, beseeching.

A gross out hologram.

The hard hand of White Hat plunged Tommy deep into their midst.

Crying, sobbing, gibbering with terror, Tommy shrank from the cloying touch of the dead. His trainers, bought by Mum, slid in the grey slime that dangled and dripped in skeins from ruptured abdomens encased in torn, orange-grey waterproofs. The sweet and sour stench choked Tommy's respiratory passages to the extent that he hardly dared breathe.

The faces of the dead stared.

They bore every expression of rage and recrimination he'd ever evoked or imagined.

'Noo-oo!'

As Tommy writhed to escape the malevolent stares of accusation, his struggles dislodged a cadaver. It fell across his young, wriggling torso, entrapping him within the hard, merciless touch of rigor mortis, and the sweet, fetid smell of unjustified death.

'No! I didn't mean —'

In the cab of the truck, the black, petrol-fire charred hand of the driver's mate slipped, disturbed by the tiny vibrations caused by the struggling youth trapped within the wrecked chassis of the truck.

A transistor radio fell from the precarious grip.

The radio burst into life with an old refrain. Like an audio ghost, the trumpet of Harry James pierced the drab, colour drained horror. A Forties-style songstress sang with the cloying sweetness of a forgotten era.

'Didn't mean to do it . . . I didn't mean to do it . . .'

***

The alien sounds from the depths of the wood disturbed the barn owl again from its early morning slumber. The head twitched. Eyes widened with the suddenness of a predator, pupils contracting against the pale daylight that filtered through the pewter, frozen foliage.

It fluttered its wings, unable to identify the source of the noise, ascending briefly above the canopy of its wooded domain, tawny head twisting. Above, the sun was a pale disk made watery by the haze. The moon looked down confusingly with its humanoid, cratered features, as though unaware that it should go.

The owl sank in terror, winged its way through the trees. It swooped low over the grass strip and the expanse of mud. Afraid of open space, it sheered away from the snort of the pale horse, and the two human figures, to fly along the house fronts, over the roofs. It finally settled opposite a bedroom window which framed a pallid shape.

Human.

***

Nude, Lucille peered through the window. She pulled a face at the owl that had just alighted on the opposite roof. The owl blinked back at her, then made a lazy, contemptuous take-off.

Lucy viewed the backs of the uninhabited dwellings with disappointment. She'd been hoping for some signs of life. Perhaps male eyes were zeroing on her right now, unable to believe their luck. Just in case, she raised her arms posily and rearranged her curls, pressing back her young shoulders so that her nipples almost touched the cold glass. Then she yawned, projecting the casual boredom that lads always seemed to interpret as a challenge, the dick heads; yawned till she stretched on tiptoe, skin goose-pimpling.

The crunch of boots on cinders made her freeze. She opened her eyes in mid-yawn, gap-toothed smile emerging. Her antennae was twitching. Frowning slightly, she concentrated fully, sought with her eyes. Like the owl. Like a predator.

Green wellingtons strode on the cinders scattered between the garden plots of clay and mud. They protected the wearer's suit from the mud splashes as the sheepskin car coat kept him proof against the lancing cold. A pale hand clutched a clipboard to his chest.

The white hardhat might have been worn due to Company Rules, but made the wearer smile because of its rakish image, she

45

could tell. And when he obviously caught sight of the naked girl in the back bedroom window, his smile grew broader still.

***

Mary ducked her head as the owl swooped. Her hand flew to her throat. There was a chilling familiarity about the old milkman. It shone through the tragic disfigurement and the contorted croak.

'Why are you here?'

Mary's jaw froze. Words could barely escape her constricted throat. They queued, caused her to choke.

'Y-you're d e a d.'

Memory.

The crew photograph in its silver frame next to Pope John Paul. It had been taken during WW2, just before the Hamburg raids — July, 1943. Dad was on the edge of the group, the single, winged AG brevet just visible on the left breast of his blue tunic.

His very outline was burned indelibly into her mind.

The milkman was a bowed, bent version.

The features, of course, were unrecognisable.

There was something else. Most air crew photos had been taken in front of their aircraft: the Lancasters, Halifaxes, Stirlings and Wimpey Wellingtons of 1943.

Dad's crew had elected to stand at the main gate of their station.

Its sign was right there above Dad's head — fuzzy monochrome, but just readable.

RAF CASTERLECK.

Mouth locked open, Mary watched the milkman shuffle forward. One of the leather gauntlets stretched out to her, palm upward. The scarred voice box leaked guttural air.

'*Mary . . .*'

Shaking with fear, she scrabbled in her purse for her rosary. Disjointed words spilled from her tremulous lips as she shrank.

'You are in the form of . . .'

The leather gauntlets gently clasped her squirming fingers. They had the cold cling of the dead. The hoarse whisper discharged from the half grinning features.

'The Antichrist is not in this place. Not in any form.'

Mary, still recoiling, forced words out. 'W-what is Casterleck?'

The ravaged face retained its lopsided grin — half scarred, half skeletal. 'Study your Old English, Mary. Caster means camp. Leck is a field of corpses. Hmph. Appropriate . . .'

Mary shot fearful glances in every direction in case there were other abominations. Only the part built house units gazed back with eyeless curiosity.

The square tower reared against the dull sky more distinctly now that the mist was clearing. Its rail was lined with tiny figures. Some were topped with pale yellow blobs — the hardhats of the construction workers. Others wore peaked caps, or leather helmets like the milkman.

Mary's mouth worked as she fingered her rosary. 'It isn't Hell?'

'No, no, Mary. Nor is it Heaven.'

She stared in holy terror at the abomination as it whispered on.

'Fools, Mary. They are not entirely responsible for their mortal deeds. They cannot be justly punished in Purgatory. Neither can they be rightly received in Heaven or in Hell . . .'

As the scarred milkman grinned his half grin in the part light, Mary remembered words from Sunday School. '*Limbus Fatuorum?* I thought only the newborn . . .'

The abomination clapped its cold gauntlets together in con-gratulation. 'Get into the cart, my child. I'll show thee . . .'

Mary Carter remained rooted in the mud fingering her rosary. The gentle breeze that had lifted the mist toyed with her head scarf. On the balcony of the distant tower, the strange collection of men watched. In front of her, the scarred milkman lifted his hands in their cold gauntlets and croaked through his half grin.

'You are an ordinary woman who is without real sin, Mary. I don't know why you are here.'

From the front of the cart the pale horse looked round at her. It rolled a baleful eye.

'Come, let us find out, my child.'

Mary inched toward the familiar shape; allowed him to help her onto the cart. At a twitch of the reins, the cart horse nodded its head and pulled between the shafts. Slowly, the wheels moved . . .

***

Less than fifty metres away, Matt Ryland marched purposefully along one of the cinder paths between the garden plots. The row he was inspecting had frames fitted at the rear. That was some-thing — much of the rest had empty sockets yawning at him as though laughing.

Judiciously, he ticked the box marked Windows on his inspec-tion sheet then peered further along the backs — ground level, upper level.

The girl was standing at one of the bedroom windows, as naked as the day that she was born. For a few seconds, Ryland considered the possibility of a Freudian illusion. The girl was straightening her long curls, yawning the way youngsters seemed to at everything. The flawless, lithe youth of her physique suggested sixteen.

When the penny dropped that she was real, Ryland grinned broadly. He scribbled in the space marked on the inspection sheet as Additional Comments, making a very careful note of the address, counting doors, reciting house numbers. Triumphantly, he turned on his heel to retrace his steps armed with his discovery of Possible Cause of Delay.

Then stopped.

The girl was still preening herself in the window. For a split second, she made eye contact. It was strange. Looking into those eyes; it was as though she knew the secrets of the universe. She went right on combing her hair, staring at him, like a landlocked mermaid luring lubbers to God knew what.

She was using an Afro comb, yawning, stretching her creamy arms, breasts undulating with that built in suspension that had defied scientific and artistic interpretation through the ages.

Ryland tapped his pencil on his inspection sheet. Faster and faster. Until it became a blur.

As his feet were drawn across the cinders to the garden plot, he suddenly used the pencil. Next to the address he added: Further Investigation — carried out . . .

THREE

THE pale horse pulled the milk cart slowly nearer the centre of New Casterleck Estate. Mary Carter pulled up her coat collar against the grey rawness. Above the rooftops the tower loomed, its silent watchers leaning, clustering, on the rail in disturbing curiosity.

Beside Mary, the milkman waved a cold leather gauntlet, black from ancient scorching. '*Limbus Infantum* is where unbaptised infants enjoy their inferior blessedness. There is *Limbus Patrum*, where dwell the prophets . . .'

Mary listened to the reminders of her faith, her skin cooling.

'Your own term, *Limbus Fatuorum*, is absolutely correct, my dear — Limbo itself being an all encompassing term to cover all departments. It was first used not so long ago, actually: thirteenth century I believe by a certain Thomas Aquinas.'

Like a living nightmare, the abomination turned to Mary in his wooden seat with his grisly half grin.

'You are unique in these times, my child, in your steadfast faith. I believe you may have caused a blip in the system. I must repeat that according to criteria you should not be in the substandard Paradise of Fools . . .'

Mary Carter stared at the abomination in terrible realisation. 'You're real, aren't you?'

The skeletal features emitted huffs of throatless amusement over the reins. 'Dear child! Just because even simple folk have lost their belief in the laid down procedures of centuries due to the out-pourings of men of mortal science, who have the conceit to lay claim to the sole access to Knowledge, does not mean the said pro-cedures have disappeared.'

A cold gauntlet waved in emphasising gesture.

'In the overall scheme of Eternity, lost faith is but an aberra-tion, heh-heh. A hiccup!'

And the pale horse nodded as it clip-clopped on its way.

***

As Lucille Carter flicked and teased her brown curls with the long Afro comb, she slyly watched the man in the suit and the white hardhat march across the mud and cinders to the back door.

Her tongue sneaked between her teeth. Her toes cringed and curled in anticipation of his knock.

When it came, a guffaw burst from her. Her eyes remained steadfastly open. The Afro comb fell to the carpet. For a second, she considered opening the door just like she was: naked.

Ooh, sorr-ee. Thought it was Mum.

That would be a giggle.

No. Hurriedly, she pulled on her towelling robe, tying it loosely. She crept to the door of Mum and Dad's room, listened, fled lithely down the new, creaking stairs, barefoot.

They were funny houses. The kitchen was at the front — dinette and lounge at the back. All the downstairs doors had retaining springs and shut by themselves when they were shoved enough for the rubber wheel to engage with the inverted U of the bracket.

The man.

He rantanned on the door again, the sound rebounding thinly off the surrounding shells of pebble-dash. The back door had a frosted glass panel, and Lucy couldn't weigh the man up properly. Tommy would scoff, saying the fact that he wore trousers guaranteed he'd be OK. Huh.

He was mature without being old. His stomach was flat. He was dead adult. Mm.

Lucy was standing in the dinette, the back door facing her. She raised her fingertips to her spreading lips as the man peered through the distorting bubbles of the glass. His hands looked cool. Like his voice.

'Hello? Council Housing Department. Are you the occupier?'

Lucy sidled up to the frosted glass, cheeks burning. She turned the brand new aluminium handle. The door was locked. Shit! The key still lay on the carpet where Dad must have pushed it through the crack of the part open window after leaving for the boring depot.

Squeaking with excitement, she snatched it up.

The man smiled through the open doorway. His teeth were flawless and he had a dimpled chin. The adult swell of his shoulders and physique made her feel weak.

'Good morning, Madam. Just making sure the house is officially occupied. I, ah, see you have the official key. Are you the tenant?'

Lucille displayed her gap toothed smile. 'Come in, then.'

'Well, ah, I have muddy boots on.'

'Take 'em off, eh?'

'Is your mother in?'

She swung her shoulders and peered at him the way the super bitches on the soaps did. 'No.'

The man looked in several directions at once. 'Well, there's no, ah, dire necessity to actually effect entry, if you see what I mean . . .'

'Eh?'

'I can see the house is officially occupied.' He held up his silly clipboard like a shield. 'If you would just furnish me with your name.'

'Lucy. I'm Lucy. Hi . . .'

'Your second name would be most appreciated, Miss, ah . . .'

'Why don't ya stop waffling and come in for a cuppa, yeah? Mum'll be out looking for the shops. She'll be back. You must be dying for it . . .'

Broad smile spreading, the man entered clutching pen and clipboard. 'Tea would be most welcome, actually, Miss, ah . . .'

Lucy held his eyes as he politely removed his green wellingtons, then she filled the kettle at the sink with a roar. She looked over her shoulder at him.

Still in the adjoining dinette, the man grinned. 'I'm Matt Ryland, Construction Management. Have you, ah, any complaints?'

Lucy simpered dreamily over her shoulder, kettle overflowing. 'I think my tits are too small.'

***

Out in Mangle Street, Frank Carter gaped back through the doors of Old Casterleck Bus Depot. The figure of the silently standing bus conductor looked deformed. Flat. When Frank edged closer he could see why.

'You're giving yourself the screaming mimis for nowt, Frank!'

Embarrassed, he walked past the engraved mirror.

The mirror was an ornate curio whose silvered surface was decorated by the portrait of a bus conductor about to issue a ticket to the touted for customer from his arcane Ultimate ticket machine. Alongside the portrait was a slogan.

Have you brushed your uniform and polished your shoes?

Remember: you represent the Charon Road Car Co. Ltd.

Established 1928.

Frank Carter pushed his way through the door marked CONDUCTORS' ROOM — a polished, brass plate. On the cream painted wall, a wood-housed clock with a plain white face displayed the time: 0510. Behind glass was a duty board. Frank peered closely and read: S/O 0520 — 11 Duty — RB 011 — Route 111 — Dep: 0530.

A hatch, locked, connected with the Cash Office and the Inspectorate. In the corner was an obsolete drop safe with quaint instructions, worn pale green paint, a wooden box for short men to stand on.

The counting table was old, as was the nest of wooden lockers next to the safe, all but one with, oddly, modern combination locks. The unlocked one bore harsh stencilling: SPARE ALMEX.

Frank shook his head, half grinning. Almexes had been phased out a decade before in most companies. This was, of course, the backwoods. Paradoxically, they'd be used to the pre-war style of running privatised bus companies.

He looked at his watch, a digital: 0512.

The Carter family had been in the backwoods just over fourteen hours.

A hardwood rack contained waybills — no computerised Wayfarer-style interface modules here. He took one, in awe that it was designed for the Almex ticket machine he'd used as a raw recruit.

Thinking of the striped bundle in the dark, lonely road, and Reg's insidious persuasion, he started to fill it in . . .

0520 floated on the liquid crystal display of his watch. No-one had arrived. Frank opened the Spare locker and found the familiar brown box, rather like an old fashioned miniature suitcase. Opening it, he popped open the aluminium case of the Almex and checked the ticket roll. Inside the box was a waybill with verified starting numbers inked in red. He screwed up the form he'd started and wrote in his own details in black biro, copying journey details from the Running Board he'd found in the appropriate rack.

In the garage, the bus allocated for this early split duty was at the front, next to the ghostly mirror. It was an old Atlantean, a quarter of a century old at least. It had a tiny door at the front and a wide sliding exit door in the middle — the first semi-auto designed for OMO — one man op. Frank started it up so the air could build to 80 psi. Beneath the brass tap at the front shutters was a watering can, much dented. As black exhaust gas billowed to the roof, he bashed open the chrome radiator cap at the nearside rear of the bus, frowning when the radiator took two cans.

He checked his watch again. All bus men lived by the clock. 0530.

He hurried back to the conductors' room. No way was he going to be late starting an unfamiliar route. The green Bakelite phone bore an instruction: Outside Line — Dial 7.

He couldn't even get a dialling tone.

In the cab of the smoking Atlantean, he tested both doors, on foot pedal and gear select. 0532.

He drove off.

The light remained on in the conductors' room. Frank's discarded waybill lay in the bottom of the green metal litter bin. With an audible creak, it opened slowly, like a flower.

The clock on the wall remained on 0510.

***

Matt Ryland could scarcely believe his luck. He was lying in the girl's bed in the otherwise empty house. She was on top, curls swaying as she rode him intently.

Slyly, she'd dropped the catch on the front door and had turned the key in the back, despite her haste.

That gap toothed grin had done it — turning from the sink, opening her towelling robe, then exhibiting the grin.

The eyes too. They never blinked. In case they missed something.

He'd dropped the clipboard.

She'd dropped the robe.

Upstairs, she'd climbed aboard like Calamity Jane, nympho extraordinary. The hair swayed. All of her swayed. The way she pressed her shoulders back and kept right on grinning at him just took his breath. Already they'd worked out a personal body language. If he gritted his teeth and widened his eyes in alarm, she stopped.

Their hands were interlaced like dancers' at the Royal Ballet. Not one word passed between them. It was all too much, too natural, too basic, too primitive for boring words.

Would you Adam and Eve it!

And the best part was that he'd probably stumbled across a major cause of the construction delay. OK, it would have taken more than one raving nymphomaniac, however enthusiastic, to throw the New Casterleck programme so far behind, but it was enough to make Doyle get the stick out.

Funny though. They were a good gang . . .

Eventually, Ryland could last no longer.

'Jesus!'

The gap toothed grin never slipped as he released several work laden weeks of pent up tension and passion. The bed shuddered, and she just grinned down at him, meowing, 'Yeah?' over and over in taunting, rhetorical askings, serpent's tongue showing between the carnivorous teeth, predatory eyes never winking.

'Have you?' he gasped. 'Did —?'

Her taunting became a contented hiss.

'I can wait. Just lie still.'

She just sat up there, a smirking victor, as if a one sided contest had taken place between a mere mortal and a . . .

In the end, he stirred.

The grin fell from her face. 'Where you off?'

'I, ah, have got work to do. Urgent. Sorry.'

The huntress' eyes glared.

His lips parted.

Exuding an old disappointment, she got off, child-woman hands sliding over his pectoral and abdominal muscles one last hungry time. Her leg, creamy-grey in the wan light, poised reluctantly in ballet-like arabesque.

Ryland lay for seconds, not daring to breathe. She did what the flesh pot video producers called, "a mandatory, irrelevant buttwalk", to the door. Here, she paused; peered angrily over her shoulder at him, talons sliding over the fresh paint work.

Then left. Like smoke . . .

Dressed, Ryland hunted around for his clipboard, hardhat and rubber boots, snatching them up fussily from the dinette carpet where they'd been dropped. The white robe was still crumpled on the kitchen tiles like discarded packaging.

'Hello?'

He called through the yawning lounge doorway. There was no answer. Up the stairwell, even the air hung, grey, static, loaded. He remembered there'd been no creaking when the girl had floated from the bedroom. She had to be in the bathroom.

He listened for running water to break the oppressive silence.

'See you!' He called, opening the front door, fumbling nervously with the dropped catch. Clicks resounding emptily, he added to the open stairwell, 'You're out of this world . . .'

Outside, he was about to march in vigorous triumph back to the site when he found something moist and sticky in the side pocket of his business suit.

His used sheath.

'Jesus, Mary and Joseph!'

Embarrassed, he looked around wildly, embedded it carefully in the mud, wiping his hands fastidiously on a man-sized tissue.

Yet he was unable to resist gazing up in wonder at the bedroom window as he retraced his steps, crunching the cinders. Twice he turned his head.

At the last moment, a female form drifted purposefully across the window frame. Ryland grimaced. He caught the impression of anger. She'd put on a clingy dress of black and white stripes.

It made her look older.

Different.

Ryland was halfway back to the site cabin when the real difference about her struck him.

Hair.

In place of the tumbling curls of chestnut brown that had entranced him so was a flowing halo of straight hair.

Blonde.

***

You made me love you . . .

The Forties' refrain cut as suddenly as it had begun. Tommy Carter peeked from among the frozen corpses of the construction gang in the wood and saw, through the splintered remains of the toppled site cabin, that White Hat had hooked a claw into the cab of the mangled truck. He'd switched off the fallen radio.

This left them silently alone in the mist shrouded forest.

The orange-grey cagoule moved slowly to the rear of the truck. Tommy could hear the inexorable press of the site boots on the damp vegetation.

Cringing away, Tommy put his hand on the cold material of a dead labourer's donkey jacket. The blue tinged lips parted to emit a tired moan as a gastric bubble was finally released in a fetid cloud.

'Mum! Mummy!'

The dead faces glared in petrified rage as the miscreant juvenile cowered in their midst. The white hardhat leaned ominously into the back of the truck, the face beneath its brim a charcoal smudge of horror. The cagoule creaked with the deliberation of the movement.

'I didn't mean to wreck the truck, Mister. It wasn't my fault. I'll never never never ever ever ever do anything wrong ever again, Mister. Honest! I'm really really honestly dead truthfully sorry, Mister. Sorry sorry sorry . . .'

The brim of the white hardhat tilted. The guttural croak sounded like a pronouncement of the dead.

'*M a y b e.   M a y b e   n o t.*'

Tommy squirmed among the dead men. 'I'm really sorry, Mister. Can't you tell by how fantastically shit scared I am?'

The rasping vocalisation wheezed again.

'*N o.*'

For all his fearful wriggling and scrabbling among the cold limbs and torsos, Tommy could not escape the hard questing hand of White Hat. Within seconds, he was being dragged through the cold forest, back towards the estate.

***

Frank drove through the grey light down to the pitifully small bus terminus in the centre of Old Casterleck. It was the cobbled forecourt of the Hanging Ditch public house.

Frank chuckled at the sheer Gothic quality of the pub sign hanging in the mist. Dutifully, he opened the narrow front door on the foot pedal. The aluminium Almex he'd slipped onto the stainless steel topped machine stand. He now ensured the flat securing bar was tight on the butterfly nut, zeroed the numbers with the plastic moulded handle. The saloon and destination light switches were down on the control panel, cramped awkwardly at his right side.

All his checks he could do by touch again. The Atlantean was the model in use when he'd learned as a young man.

A man was standing in the doorway.

Frank must have missed him in the fog, unless he'd been huddled in the old wooden shelter. He had one foot on the step.

No. A clog. The real thing — with an iron shod wooden sole, shining rivets winking in the cab light. The man was rummaging in an old hessian bag that hung from his shoulder.

Rummaging.

Slowly.

The man was very pale for an outdoor rustic. His skin was like dried vellum, as though he'd been standing in a museum all night displaying the clothes of the nineteenth century: striped granddad shirt with no collar, black waistcoat, neckerchief that did not look foppish.

Slowly.

Hairs rose on the back of Frank's neck as his initial amusement faded. Slowly, the rustic's eyes rose to meet his. At the same time, his vellum hand lifted something out of the hessian bag.

The movements seemed coordinated to a totally different time dimension.

Frank felt goose pimples spread over his flesh like a plague virus as he watched the unfolding actions. He was afraid of their culmination.

What had he taken out of the hessian bag?

The faraway eyes focused. The mouth opened with the impossibly slow intention to speak. The vellum hand had now cleared the bag, the length of the fingers slowly rubbing the hem. It was holding something. Not coins. The clog remained on the step. The words, when they emerged, were slowly enunciated as the vellum fingers placed some objects on the curved cash tray.

Two eggs.

'*Hast tha seen my cow?*'

Frank fought an impulse to laugh, to shriek in relief. The two eggs had soft, downy feathers adhering to their shells. They were warm to the touch. Frank swallowed, compressed his lips.

'Saw a black one near the crossroads.'

The rustic's face lit up as slowly as the rising sun.

'*Thank ee!*'

The other clog rose languidly to the step of the platform.

Eventually, Frank was able to drive off. But he still felt waves of musty cold down his left side and shoulder, as though a dread hand was slowly squeezing, claiming his tissues, muscles and nervous system. At the crossroads, the black cow meekly allowed the man to lead it away.

At the next stop were a group of weeping women all dressed in black shawls and clogs. In their midst was a priest.

The women all held tightly robed babies.

***

When Lucille discovered that the mature man in the suit had lost interest in her as quickly as the boys she normally craved, she ran a bath.

Mum would shout when she came back for wasting gas on hot water. Useless explaining she had to wipe the slate clean.

It was only when Lucy immersed herself in the clinging warmth to relax in the soporific steam that she was able to sense The Presence.

Probably, it was wishful thinking.

It was fun larking with Tommy, giggling when he landed in the shit, but it was she who always bore the brunt. She was the Big Sister. Mum had always told her: you are your brother's keeper.

Huh. Keeper . . .

The Keeper was there to take the can, right? If only she was the one who had the Big Sister: someone she could pour out her troubles to, who'd listen without mocking or lecturing about getting bored and pissed off.

She'd be tall and blonde.

This was so they could be told apart. Lucy could almost see the two of them. Tangible — the blonde one, and the curly haired sister who could then wriggle out of the brown stuff.

The blonde one was older, wiser, kind.

And on her side!

What name could she have?

Vicky.

Cool.

Vicky wore clingy dresses, and was always making herself over to go out with the men who always fell at her feet. Vicky was no threat, though, because she had the men, and Lucy had the boys. Yes! The only argument they'd have would be about who got to take a bath first, yeah? Baths were the thing. The being clean thing gave you confidence. Mum always said: cleanliness was next to Godliness. OK? And you had to take a bath after, too, to make a fresh start — because none of them wanted you for keeps. Everything was for The Moment. So the trick was to give, like, a string of Moments . . .

So, the steam rose from her glowing, alive body to hang in a shroud just below the ceiling.

Then the smile fled from Lucille's face. She'd broken The Rule. She'd had one of The Men. The Men belonged to Vicky.

The door.

The bathroom door had the same kind of aluminium handle as all the other doors in the house — and all the frigging doors in school, too. It felt like she'd never left School, like it was haunting her.

The door handle was turning ever so slowly. Downwards.

Lucy had not bothered bolting the bathroom door. If Mum came in, they were all girls, right? If Dad came in, unawares, she'd laugh at the way he'd say 'Shit' and cover his eyes and back out. Quaint or what? If Tommy came in, OK he'd gape the way the other boys did, as though he couldn't believe his luck — just like the Grownup Man in the suit.

He'd been no different. Stronger. Musky sea smell. And he'd been in just as big a hurry to get away from her before he got caught as the rest. Asshole.

So why had she taken one of the Men?

They were Vicky's . . .

The bathroom door handle had reached the bottom of its travel, spring squeaking inside the lock. The bathroom door opened.

The shroud of steam filtered away through the ever widening gap. Funny. Lucy could hear the bottom of the junk wood frame scraping across the pile of the carpet Dad had laid last night just to please Mum.

Maybe they should have stayed to help him.

Sure enough, it was who Lucy thought it was. She just knew. Vicky.

The blonde hair hung like a straight curtain as she turned to close the door behind her. She was wearing a clingy wool number in black and white stripes.

So real.

Lucy could even hear the ball catch click as Vicky closed and bolted the door; could even see her nail polish glitter as she manipulated the little silver bolt.

Which was why Lucy said, 'Hi, Vicky.'

None of it could possibly be real, of course. Yet she could hear the boiler rumble as the gas ignited again at the whim of the thermostat.

The blonde hair splayed as Vicky turned her face toward her.

Lucy's jaw fell in shock.

Terrible scars ended in an unnatural white line where a misshapen half nose and mouth seemed to have been grafted on by a mad toy maker on acid. The side of the mouth. It was puckered. Drawn back by hastily applied tent stitches by an underpaid junior on a bad night.

The deformed fantasy —

(What else could it be but a dreamy doze in warm water gone bad?)

— walked to the bath in high heels in one, two, three quick steps, steel dinkies leaving tiny, round indentations in the pile of Dad's carpet. Painted talons reached out.

All in slick, predator action.

'Naaahooo —'

Lucille's scream turned to gurgling bubbles as the talons clawed at her neck and cheek with inhuman force. When the bubbles stopped, the threshing began. The demonic face looked more deformed from beneath the mutating, light-bending surface of the water — especially with Mum's green bubble bath in it — all the white fangs baring in maniacal fury, instead of just one knackered up side.

When spots appeared in Lucy's vision, the talons dragged her out in a pouring torrent. Lucy gasped for life-giving air, centimetres from the snarling she-cat of her nightmares.

'Sorry, sorry, sorry, Vicky! I didn't mean it. Honest. I was just curious. I couldn't help it. It's the way I'm made — aaah haaa!'

The half lips worked in gibbering fury, unanchored flaps of mouth vibrating, spears of saliva spurting as the scarred larynx issued wheezes of hate.

'*I   w a n t   y o u r   l i f e.*'

FOUR

KEITH Doyle looked round as Matt Ryland kicked open the door of the site cabin. Keith was leaning silently over the dented kettle on the canister driven gas ring.

'What did you find out?' he asked.

Ryland told him about seeing the nude girl in the window.

Doyle shrugged. 'The gang have had women all over the country. I told you, Matt, it's a combination of shit weather, shit equipment, and worst of all, shit luck.' His heavy face turned wearily as he lifted the tea mugs. 'How d'you know the girl is touting for business anyway?'

Ryland spluttered. 'There has to be some reason for what's going on here. I've never known such a delay. I have to chase. I-it's my duty to get to the bottom of things.'

Doyle's slab face was unmoved. 'Did you spot anything else?' Ryland looked at such a loss, Keith Doyle relented. 'Well you're not on your own, Matt. We've tried every trick in the book to change the run of shit luck. We've come up with zilch, too.'

Handing Ryland a steaming mug, he nodded out the window. 'Checked the weather report this morning?'

Matt shook his head.

'Moderate southwesterlies, slight chance of rain. Take a look . . .'

With Matt Ryland peering over his shoulder, Keith watched the dark hammerheads growing out of the grey blanket that invariably covered both Old and New Casterleck.

Funny. He could not remember a single sunny day. Normally, the sky was like the static backdrops in old British films made in black and white and on a shoestring. This time, even as they watched, the cloud deepened in tone until it was jet black. There was a boiling action at the base of the cumulus nimbus. The main mass of cloud reared like a pagan devil whose featureless visage glared down in unimaginable rage.

Or was it lust?

Keith fancied he could see hollow eyes forming, lengthening ears, the widening cavern of a mouth; while all the time the sheer presence of the phenomenon bore down in a tangible weight of fury and expectation, condensing the air.

'Jesus,' said Ryland, flatly.

'I don't think the good Lord would approve of this asshole.'

Because from the gaping maw that spread across the grey sky, a single bolt of lightning writhed like a living tongue — all seven miles of it. Seconds later, the ripping calico type of thunder made both construction men, who'd seen every type of weather there was, put their hands to their ears.

'By the horned toad, what have you been up to, Matt?'

'What d'you mean?'

Ryland, he noticed, was screwing the top sheet off his clipboard into a little ball.

The base of the sky monster was growing a tail. Black soot spiralled into the ground within the woods. The two men were outside the hut now. Both wore their white hardhats and were standing near the mechanical diggers whose shovels lay buried in the mud like the heads of feeding dinosaurs. Dust blew round their feet and the tracks of the vehicles. Ryland's crumpled sheet blew across the site like a tiny, bouncing toy.

There was a developing roar that made them crane their necks at the dark tail that twisted visibly above the distant trees over the housetops. Keith Doyle realised that the black haze that surrounded it like a veil was the swirl of flying debris.

'I do believe we have what is sometimes referred to as a tornado, Mr Ryland.' And then for good measure. 'Sir.'

'In this country?'

'It's been known.'

Ryland backed away, almost swallowing the cheroot that had appeared automatically between his teeth. As he began to run, Keith Doyle's voice tore through the disturbed air.

'Not in the hut.'

They raced toward the nearest tracked vehicle, a 'dozer. Leaping onto the waist high track, Doyle ripped open the cab door. Ryland scrambled in after him, yanking the door shut.

Doyle felt they were like kids, diving under the bedclothes.

The unearthly roar had increased to a shriek, like a football crowd of howling banshees. Something dark fell upon them from the sky, tangling with the grounded blade and hydraulics of the 'dozer.

It was a thirty foot birch, distinguishable to Keith by the white diamond shaped patches. The polypore fungus, conspicuous as white brackets on the trunk, had obviously ate away its inner timber. The first real gale would have felled it. This monster had uprooted it, probably after only sixty years' growth.

The cab of the 'dozer was showered briefly by its dark twigs, like an afterthought. Then the corpse was whirled on its way.

The monolith was directly overhead. There was a swift aerial bombardment of what turned out to be grapefruit sized hail. A small percentage of the 5,800 tons of water being carried by the monster rained down block size — a narrow strip that missed the hut but hit the now multi-dented cab of the 'dozer.

'Oh!' said Ryland.

Keith Doyle looked to his left. The site cabin rocked wildly on its brick piles. The roof blew off like a shed skin. The walls were whirled away with little resistance.

As Ryland gulped behind his forgotten cheroot, Doyle explained in a deadpan shout the kind of data that modern management delighted to hide behind.

'The inner winds of a tornado are so fierce they can only be estimated. 200, 500 mph? The biggest is only 1600 feet across at ground level. They can pluck up people, animals, cars, trees, buildings. But the worst is the calm eye in the middle. The air inside the eye is less dense than the air outside. A tornado bulldozing quickly across a house causes the denser air inside the house to press out much harder than the air pressing in. OK?'

Ryland goggled, popeyed, from behind the cheroot. 'What does it do, Keith?'

Doyle lifted a hard hand, jerked open his fingers.

'Pouf!'

The 'dozer itself was rocking in the dried mud. Dust rose in a spiral like a sandstorm. They were in a flat calm circled by a wall of solid black. They yawned in panic to unblock their ears. Doyle felt weightless, as though he could push himself ever upward.

In the swirl, the roof of a house circled their position like an enemy aircraft.

***

The milk cart had finally clopped and squeaked to the centre of the estate. As Mary Carter watched, the dark twisting cloud passed within 300 metres before roping out, subsiding, amid houses on the far side of the compound.

Compound?

The gate was a red and white barrier. It was raised by members of the RAF Regiment. They saluted solemnly as they passed through. Their faces were very pale.

'Here we are, Pete.'

The deformed milkman handed over two bottles for the guardhouse in exchange for a small, but succulent looking, rainbow trout. Then his cold gauntlet closed over Mary's hand. She flinched into even icier shock.

'Don't,' he murmured, 'leave the cart on any account.'

The abomination shuffled into the guardroom near the checkpoint.

Mary gazed at the collection of ramshackle huts. Some were homemade shacks. Others were Nissen. They just sat on the mud, as if they'd always been there. Beyond, on the edge of the airfield, was the crashed hulk of a Lancaster bomber. Mary could identify it by the twin curves of the tailplane Father had shown her in grainy photographs. They poked up into the dead sky.

'Pranged last night, Madam.'

One of the guards stepped forward. He had sergeant's chevrons on the upper arms of his battle dress. The black bar of his moustache moved in his alabaster face beneath the slashed peak of his cap.

'They all got the chop. One missing. They're still being debriefed . . .'

Unable to answer, Mary fingered her rosary. Her lips mimed the first Hail Mary.

The cold grin of the sergeant turned from her. His ramrod figure slow-marched across to the control tower where construction crews and aviators still clustered the iron rail of the balcony. His military tones carried crisply in the drab light.

'Your foreman's coming with your oppo.'

Slowly, the construction men filed down the metal stairs on the outside of the tower. They straggled past the cart, untidy enough to cause the moustachioed sergeant to shake his head in frustration.

The striped barrier lifted.

As they passed, each of the labourers and tradesmen turned his head to look at Mary. Some hobbled badly, one having something white sticking unnaturally out of his overall. There was a squeaking sound. One of them grinned at her.

He was opening and closing a pair of stout side cutters.

As though examining evidence.

***

As the water was cooling, Lucille got out of the bath.

She'd been dozing in the bath and had woke with relief. She might have drowned. Her ears were numb. They were full of water. If she didn't know better, she could have sworn she'd actually slipped beneath the surface. Mum's green bubble bath stained the water. She'd have to buy her some more.

Fastidiously, she towelled her brown curls dry.

She pulled a disapproving face at the steamed up mirror. Despite the care she'd taken to perm the curls in, she had a sudden urge to straighten them. It was time for an image change.

Long, straight hair turned heads.

Especially *blonde*.

She did, in any case, feel different.

Wrapped tightly in the towel, Lucy hurried to the bedroom. She checked her stride, making herself walk. Gracefully. She snorted with annoyance when she saw the crumpled state of the duvet. Fussily, she straightened it, patting the corners, making sure the studs were fastened.

The towel fell. Grimacing at her careless exhibition, she drew the curtains. The thought of being peeped at made her blush as she climbed hurriedly into her striped mini dress.

***

The weeping women huddled at the bus stop in their black shawls. The babies they held in their arms were quiet and still. They had white faces, like dolls.

Frank Carter pulled the bus up as close as he could, despite the isolated stop being overgrown with couch grass and cow parsley. Smiling deferentially, he pressed the pedal to fold open the small entrance door.

Each woman was weeping in the fatalistic way the casts of old Italian movies affected. Each woman asked for the church, the next stop, then filed through as though participating in some long established piece of theatre, or country ritual.

The final passenger was the priest.

A Catholic priest in flowing black cassock.

The priest smiled formally; nodded with what Frank identified as connected reality. A high blown phrase, it just appeared in his mind.

'Eight of us, please, driver. 'Tis only one stop.'

'Two pounds forty, Father,' said Frank.

'Ah!' sighed the priest philosophically — or was it fatalistically? 'The price of death!'

The priest paid with cash that included a freshly minted, two pound coin not yet fully familiar to Frank with its twin coloured alloys. Automatically, Frank worked the mechanical lever rapidly, producing a growing streamer of ticket roll. He wasn't going to do an all-in-one ticket till the depot got used to him.

Mystified, he pulled away in first, snatch changing to second and lifting the accelerator after sufficient delay to take the jerk out of the old, air operated gearbox. Ahead, the stolid spire of the church was already poking above the two metre high couch grass that bordered all the fields.

He glanced briefly in the internal mirror. The women snivelled in the washed out light. Two seconds was enough to reveal what struck Frank as the most odd.

The women were comforting each other.

The babies were clutched safely to their bosoms right enough, but were not the object of their commiserations.

The white, dolls' faces lolled in the wan daylight.

At the rear of the saloon, the priest in black made eye contact through the mirror with a dry smile that was as submissive to Fate as the ritual tears of the women. Which made Frank look away.

He pulled up gently outside the church. Its door was open despite the overgrown state of its short gravel drive. Frank flicked the selector into the exit door slot, causing the characteristic hiss and rumble as it slid back on its greased rod.

The women filed out obediently with their staring, unwinking babies. The priest nodded back through the door.

'Thank you, my son. Blessed be.'

In the nearside wing mirror, the images of the women collected by the church gate, nodding to the priest who, cassock billowing, led them through like a shepherd, head upraised; on his face, a whimsical smile . . .

Just before the turn for the New Casterleck estate, a figure staggered out of the trees. It wore long boots and a leather bomber jacket. He fell to his knees, and Frank muttered, 'Every one a gem.'

With bowed head, the man waved a hand, almost in despair.

Frank shook his head at the suspect drunk, marvelling at his ability to find the juice so early in the morning. He relented and pulled in, pedalled the narrow door open.

Grimy hands were placed either side of the entrance. The man's hair, though stiff with dirt, was parted neatly in the middle.

'All right, mate?' Frank watched, warily.

The man hung for a second in the grey. Then he lifted his head.

Frank grimaced. The side of the face was scraped red raw, to the extent that an eyebrow and half the moustache were missing. The undamaged flesh was black with soot and oil. Teeth revealed themselves in a rueful smile.

Frank got out of the cab and helped the man to a seat.

'Had an accident, mate?'

The man smiled again. He dug a hand inside the fleecy collar of his bomber jacket. Frank waved away the attempt to pay. The man's voice was gentle, almost cheerful. Indomitable.

'One could safely assume such, old boy. We caught a packet.'

Frank frowned. We . . . 'Where you going, mate? Do you want medical attention?'

'Not far to go, you see, good sir.' A finger of determination wagged. 'Under one's own steam, you know. Matter of principle and all that.'

Engaging gear, Frank watched him through the mirror. The man was sprawling with exhaustion and discomfort in the front seat, but with the persistent stoic smile, grimy hand continuing to claw inside the jacket. Finally, it emerged with a torn piece of leather, broken goggles, a length of lead with a Bakelite jack plug trailing. Bits of smashed lens from the goggles tinkled to the platform.

'Oh damn . . .'

More digging inside the jacket . . . At last, he came up with a twisted stick of barley sugar. Frank could hear the crackle of the transparent sweet paper as it was unwrapped.

The bus was now approaching the next stop on the estate ring road. The man stretched out a black hand, fingers clawing for the support pole. Grunting, he heaved himself to his feet. Frank started the big exit door sliding open then went to help him down to the roadway mud. The scraped leather of the jacket reeked of petrol.

'Will you be OK?'

'Sweet as a nut, old boy!'

Franked watched him lurch across the mud. Despite the limp and facial injuries, he looked vaguely familiar, yet impossibly unreal at the same time.

Staying in third gear to negotiate the ruts, Frank caught sight of a grey smudge looming above the rooftops: some sort of square tower structure. Had to be in the centre of the estate.

The staggering man had looked like a character in an old black and white British film. Was that what seemed familiar? Also, most people Frank knew made everybody aware if they were hurt, possibly to play the compensation game. This guy seemed determined to shrug it off, as if he accepted such penalties for his way of life, whatever it was.

Frank scanned the half built houses almost desperately for signs of life. There were none — just a feeling of dread isolation. And there was a wide swathe leading through the houses where scarcely anything stood, as though a giant child had skidded his seven league foot through to leave a path of destruction. Had it been there when he'd passed in the van earlier? He thought not.

On the other side of the road, in the woods, was a similar gap. A fire break? Close to this was a group of building workers, yellow hardhats clustering, as if someone were dishing up grub in the open . . .

Ahead, something moved in the, as yet, glassless shelter.

A girl in a striped dress.

Cold memory made his stomach tighten as he stared — until he saw the familiar brown curls cascading to the shoulders.

Frank pressed the front door open. 'Where the hell are you going, Lucille?'

His daughter's voice sounded different.

'The hairdressers.'

***

From the milk cart, Mary Carter watched the red and white barrier lower behind the silently filing workmen. They disturbed her so much she bit her lip. And there was the coldly smiling manner of the regimental guard sergeant. He seemed to share a secret with them. Knowledge.

A Nissen hut door burst open and a squad of WAAFs formed up in the dried mud. A corporal screamed at them about Dressing, and there was a shuffle of black, sensible shoes. Mary frowned. She remembered the twinge of sadness she'd felt on behalf of her father when the TV news had announced the disbandment of the women's separate force — all mucked and messed together now. Yet here they all were, wearing the rather shapeless peaked caps of more than half a century ago.

With increasing disquiet, Mary watched them march by in the insubstantial light.

Their face were old, wrinkled vellum. Withered. Crones. They were all old crones, as proud and ingenuous as they looked . . .

The guardroom door opened and closed. The milkman hobbled toward her through the same grey with his skeletal half grin. In his gauntlet fluttered a telex flimsy.

'They know about you, but records are incomplete. I am to take you to the station commander under escort. Let us hope . . .'

The cart lurched beneath his weight as he clambered up beside her. Somehow, she'd expected it wouldn't, as though they were all ethereal images trapped in a Lewis Carroll style dream.

The guard sergeant climbed into the back. Smiling in his whimsical way, the sergeant perched on a galvanised metal crate and took out his issue revolver, its lanyard dangling from the large ring attached to the knurled butt. Breaking it, he loaded brass rounds into its chamber, one by one, smile constant beneath his dark moustache and slashed peak.

Outside a large Nissen hut, the deformed milkman helped Mary down from the cart, patting her shoulder optimistically. The sergeant marched them down a beeswaxed corridor where they had to wait beside pinned up aircraft recognition diagrams. These showed plan, side and front elevations of old, prop driven aircraft.

From beyond a closed door came the hum of male voices, then the sergeant reappeared.

'Enter!'

The station commander had four broad rings round the cuffs of his blue tunic. At his left breast was the winged brevet that Father had said meant Pilot. Beneath it was a double row of unfamiliar campaign medals, headed by the stripes of the AFC.

On the desk, beside a much doodled upon blotter, was a pewter model of a back-to-front looking biplane.

The grey haired officer had the face and build of a small monkey.

The sergeant stamped his boot. 'Mrs Mary Carter, sir!'

Mary flinched, but the station commander's face lit up like a mini sun. His smile of greeting exposed oversized teeth as he looked up from the slim file before him.

'Sergeant, find a chair for Mrs Carter.'

'Sir!'

Boots thudded. Doors crashed.

'I'm Group Captain Gabriel, Mrs Carter. I'm in charge of this establishment.'

His voice was soft, but carried an inherent authority that prevented Mary from actually applying a term like Gentle. Head teachers made her feel this way: the priest, Father when he was alive. Consequently, she clasped her hands before her, dark head bowed.

'Am I in some sort of trouble?' she asked.

The monkey smile broadened into a laugh. 'Certainly no more than the rest of us.' He unfolded a pair of horn beam spectacles and slipped them on his nose. One of the arms was bound by black insulation tape.

The sergeant crashed back in and placed a metal, folding chair just behind her — her for the use of. She could sense him Standing At Ease behind her, the bar of the moustache stretching slightly with an expectant little grin.

'Wait outside, Sergeant.'

'Sir!'

Group Captain Gabriel smiled wryly, as though the noise and formality of military correctness were designed to amuse him. He spread a hand, indicating that she sit.

'This is your file, Mrs Carter. It contains your name, your address in what's laughingly considered the Real World — isn't that what they refer to it as nowadays . . .?'

Perching on the hard chair, knees together, Mary nodded, like a church mouse.

'There are the usual cross reference codes for your immediate family . . .' He pulled toward him some considerably thicker files. 'We have all the data we need on those. They are what you might call, concrete examples of criteria . . .'

The warm smile convinced Mary that she was to speak. 'I. Er. Concrete . . .?'

'Concrete indeed! Archetypal, you might say. Our purpose in this establishment, you see, is to determine the concrete aspects of that indefinable quality known as Human Nature.' He chuckled, teeth and eyes like the sun in the grey. 'The contemporary collo-quialism for such a brief is, I believe, Mission Impossible. Yes . . .?'

Mary had to force her voice to be audible in the spartan office. 'Sir, you have details of my family?'

'Indeed!'

'Francis? Lucille? Thomas?'

The smiling group captain peered at the cross references in his slim file. Mary could see the carefully inked entries reflected in the lens of his spectacles, just above the exposed, monkey teeth. 'They are sharing the family surname of Carter — that I can confirm!'

Dread settled its cold touch on Mary's nerve ends, cooling her skin beneath her clothes. 'Are they safe, sir?'

His grin grew broader in the condensed grey.

'Please,' she whispered.

The group captain cleared his throat. 'They are as safe as they could be in this environ, Mrs Carter. Provisionally, you all come under the same classification, you see — at least, as far as we are concerned . . .'

Mary stared at the little man behind the battered desk.

The hut, the furnishings, even the little man himself: all had an air of temporary existence, as if they were designed to be swept away, temporary buildings and all, at the stroke of a ministerial pen, leaving only the vastness of the Universe.

'Please, sir, tell me what you want with them.'

The smile glowed. The diminutive officer practically rubbed his hands with approval. 'Your question does you great credit, Mrs Carter! At least, in the way it was put. Your use of the word Them rather than Us. Excellent, excellent!'

'Please, sir . . .'

Tears fought their way past her self control, which prompted the little group captain to produce a neatly pressed handkerchief from his tunic.

'My dear,' he said in his soft voice, 'allow me to help you all . . .'

***

White Hat stomped through the grey trees, boots crushing remorselessly. Tommy Carter ceased struggling to escape the inhuman grasp. What now froze him with terror was the emergence of the other shapes as they left the wood.

They were crossing a curiously flat area which gave a view of the houses. Yellow hardhats clustered round. Their angry faces were all familiar, and all the angrier now that they had regained the power of motion.

'No!' cried Tommy. 'I didn't mean —'

Some of the workmen hobbled badly. One of them was grinning in a bestial manner that caused Tommy to struggle afresh. The grin and the hands . . . The hands worked the side cutters, opening and closing them so that they squeaked.

The pale, unhinged grin grew wider with every squeak.

The flat area led across the road directly to the site. But White Hat led the ragged, menacing column along the ruined fence, past the strangely flattened couch grass, until an official looking barrier was reached — a hand operated red and white pole.

A military looking guard raised the pole.

A corporal marched out of the guardroom to meet them.

He and White Hat conversed for a few minutes, flat shapes in the morning light. Then the corporal marched across to peer at the writhing Tommy Carter.

'So this is the little beggar!'

There was a chorus of rough affirmations.

'Bring him in, the little bastard!'

'No!' cried Tommy. 'You're supposed to fetch my mum. That's what my rights are. I want my mum. Mummy!'

The corporal's ramrod back continued to march. 'Little bastards like you have no frigging rights!'

There was an outburst of enthusiastic agreement as the boy was hustled unceremoniously into the guardroom. Inside, there was a metal door leading to some animal-like cages. Someone was hammering a metal object on the bars with accompanying yells.

'Come and join us, kid! *Semper in excreta*! *Semper in* frigging *excreta*! Yee-haa!'

Ignoring the racket, the corporal seated himself behind a polished desk in the spartan front office. 'The sergeant's on escort duty. I'm filling in. Give me the facts.' He pulled a pad towards him and bent his cropped head over it.

White Hat wheezed in his blood freezing tones. 'This little bastard cut the brake line on our truck, Corporal. As a direct result, we all got the chop in the woods.'

The hard faced corporal looked up. He had a big nose that had been broken many times. 'Any survivors?'

'Not a one, Corporal!'

'So you're all officially dead?'

The disturbing rumble of growls and yeas and fierce nods of bitter consent left no possible doubt.

'Just for the record.' The corporal made a careful note. He looked up at Tommy.

The boy quailed before the merciless, hard eyes, and turned to flee. But found himself face to face with the squatting cadaver with the side cutters. The workman sniggered wildly, saliva and rheum splurging from broken jaws. Rough hands thrust him back in front of the corporal, who bent his moon face to within centimetres.

'Before my impartial judgement, what have you to say for yourself, shit brain?'

Tommy compressed his lips. The angry, cartoon faces, the rough hands that held him: all looked and felt grotesque. Unreal.

'I'm dreaming, aren't I?'

From his great height, the corporal said, 'I can assure you, young man, I'm as real as a .303 bullet . . .'

Tommy laughed. 'You're all assholes!'

There was a heart stopping yell from the cells. 'Give 'em hell, kid!'

The corporal smashed his baton against the cell bars.

'All assholes!' cried Tommy. He peered at the corporal's broken nose. 'You're an asshole!'

'Yee haa!' gurgled the unseen prisoner.

The corporal slammed his baton on the desk. 'Are you disput-ing the facts, young man?' He gestured to the workman with the unhinged look. 'Let's see the evidence.'

The side cutters were tossed onto the desk. The corporal picked them up, examined them, held them to his broken nose. 'I smell brake fluid!'

Wild clanging came from the cells. 'Feee, fiii, fooo, fummm!'

The cutters were thrust under Tommy's nose.

'All right, Mister, I did it —'

'Idiot!' yelled the beast in lockup. 'Never surrender!'

'I did it, right? I was angry 'cos the guy in the white hat smacked me when he knew he couldn't. Them days are gone, right? But . . . I didn't mean to do any harm. Honest! I'd never ever do it again, Mr Corporal, sir . . .'

On the pad, the corporal of the guard wrote: Confessed.

'Hey, wait a minute!'

The corporal nodded perfunctorily. Looking up he said, 'As we are at war, take him out for summary execution.'

'W-what?'

'Take the little bastard out and shoot him!'

Within frenetic minutes, Tommy was watching a squad of what the corporal called Erks assembled. One of them was still chewing away on something diabolical out of the cookhouse. He burped.

This made Tommy laugh, more incredulous than ever.

The erks were all issued with Lee Enfield bolt action rifles from the armoury that looked as big as themselves, along with .303 live rounds.

Tommy brayed with laughter.

His mirth was matched by that of the ragged workmen. They dragged the boy to a sandbagged enclosure at the rear of the guard-house and bound him to a post of solid looking timber. The post wasn't exactly riddled with live round discharges — nor was it entirely free of them.

The ragged workmen gathered with a look of expectancy similar to that of boys who clustered round giggling girls at the back of certain notorious outbuildings at school. They greeted each stage of the procedure with roars of rough approval — much nodding and a strange righteousness that looked as odd and out of time as everything felt.

The corporal marched across with a strip of blackout material.

'Blindfold? State Yes or No!'

'No . . . Yes . . . No. Yes. Mummy!'

The all pervading grey of the dull day changed to blackness as the corporal tied the knot at the back of his skull. Tommy wriggled and tore at his bonds. He'd had dreams like this before, enjoying the lurid and astonishingly complex detail, and the joyous release from helplessness that came on waking.

'Wake up!' he cried. 'I don't want any more. Enough, yeah? Please wake up. I'm sorry. Honest. Sorry-sorry-sorry!'

But the nightmare continued, though in sound only. Boots stamped and scraped. The hungry erk belched. Workmen's voices snarled fierce encouragement. Bolt actions clicked, snapped, rattled.

'Load!'

The bolts were rammed home with little co-ordination. There was another burp.

'Present!'

An awful silence fell. The air felt heavy enough to crush. Only the distant sound of marching could be heard, and weary screams about Dress.

'Aim!'

Further away, an aero engine whizzed and coughed into life.

FIVE

'FIRST things first, Mrs Carter.'

The group captain held up a finger, as though about to issue a special favour. He drew from his desk a form, then laid a fountain pen upon it with a mannered gesture.

'Our purpose here in this establishment is difficult to explain in contemporary terms, Mrs Carter. I find the present age regard themselves as Up Front. Oh! And there is Political Correctness!' He shook his monkey head in wonder. 'An exceedingly optimistic phrase, don't you think, Mrs Carter?'

Mary Carter stared at the officer. She could see paler greys reflected in his repaired spectacles, and smell the mud, the stale sweat, petrol. She felt if she stared any harder her eyes would fracture like glass.

'Please, sir. Have mercy. My family are only ordinary people. My husband is a bus driver. Thomas is at school. Lucille has just left and will be looking for work — anything she can get.'

Group Captain Gabriel's smile never wavered. He tilted his head over one of the thick files. 'Frank Carter?'

'Yes, sir. What have they done?'

Again, the finger rose in delight. 'Now we are getting to the point, Mrs Carter.'

'Thank the Lord!'

The smile fled from Gabriel's face. His complexion immediately lost its glow and assumed a dull grey. 'Mrs Carter!' He seemed shocked. Concerned.

Mary flinched so hard as he sprang to his feet that her hands leapt like the motor reaction of a corpse. The officer appeared content to pace up and down, like a headmaster considering the punishments at his disposal.

'Mrs Carter, I beseech you to consider carefully before using such terminology during the course of this official interview.'

Mary swallowed, opened her mouth, forced speech. 'I'm sorry, sir. I . . . . I know it is wrong to take the Lord's name in vain . . .'

'You know, then.' The statement shot like tracer from the little man. He had his hand in his tunic pocket.

Mary tried to qualify. 'One hears it so much from every quarter these days. If one lets it, it rubs off, sir.'

'Blasphemy?'

'B-Blasphemy, sir.'

'At least you have confessed to it.' The smile returned. The glow, too. Joy, almost. The group captain reseated himself behind the desk with what looked like relief.

He raised his finger again. 'Contemporary circumstances are, of course, taken into account. But only up to a point. One only has to think of our Lord in the Wilderness.'

Mary nodded vigorously. Desperately. 'There are so few believers left, sir.'

'Of course.'

'But His example is always before us.'

It was Gabriel's turn to nod vigorously. 'It's a matter of record, Mrs Carter. As is this interview. As Officer Commanding, I have certain discretion — but only up to a point.'

'Yes, sir.'

Gabriel leant forward. 'The real purpose of this establishment is known only to a few. Need to know, Mrs Carter. Need to know.'

'Yes, sir.'

'I can only hint, Mrs Carter. Diplomacy — real diplomacy — is a forgotten art . . .'

Mary stared on.

Gabriel spread is hands, voice lowering. 'I have to speak with my mouth, Mrs Carter.'

'I think I understand, sir.'

'There is black and there is white, Mrs Carter. Black and white . . . Now tell me this: what is in between?'

Mary stared long and hard. The little man beamed in a state of expectation in his little hut. Far away, she could hear the sound of doors slamming, voices, marching, running.

'Grey?'

Gabriel was overjoyed. 'The Grey Area, Mrs Carter! In some ways your contemporary age is very simplistic. People talk of the Here And Now — the only thing that matters being what you are going to do next. All decisions then boil down to Boolean Algebra.' He settled back and clasped his hands. He smiled like the sun, shook his head. 'It's only when the long term consequences are considered that life becomes not so simple. Yes?'

Not fully comprehending, but anxious, Mary nodded.

'We have considered Black and White, Mrs Carter,' he said. 'Now we must consider Right and Wrong. What is between, Mrs Carter . . .?'

***

Keith Doyle watched the dust settle. The circling roof sank into the swirling haze with a muffled crash. It blended with the boom of exploding houses as the tornado swept its dark path.

'Holy shit!' cried Matt Ryland.

Keith looked across at his reddening face, the mouth a round O of disbelief. 'Can you see what we're up against, Matt?'

'Well —'

'I knew you thought you'd found a cause when you came across that tart stripping off in that window. That is the only occupied house on the estate. You know, and I know, it'd take an awful lot of tarts stripping off in windows to screw things up to this level.'

Ryland started to back off. He patted his foreman on the shoulder. 'I'll get some experts down right away, Keith. Can you set up in one of the completed show units in the meantime?'

'You know I can, Matt. This is our bread and butter.'

The towering plume of the dark twister had finally cascaded to nothing beyond the site boundary. Only the featureless grey was left in the sky.

Doyle and Ryland climbed out of the cab of the 'dozer. Doyle wanted to feel himself all over to check he was still intact. They walked a few paces eyeing the devastation. Keith smiled grimly when Ryland's arm settled round his shoulders.

'You know you have the best gang in the Company, Keith. Why d'you think you got the job? This is the first sizeable council estate to be even contemplated in years by the lily-livered authorities. It's all been little, fiddly housing trust jobs. They had to do something to justify their existence — there's an election due.'

Keith looked at him hard. 'So you reckon they'll want to go on — even after this?'

Ryland paled. He was thinking of blustering, Keith could tell. Finally, he said, 'They're committed, Keith — promises made, and so on. There is such a thing as severe weather cover. Even if they fudge that, they'll still have to underwrite. Muddle through, Keith, boy. Muddle through . . .'

***

'**Muddling** through, Mrs Carter. That's what we do, as a nation. This is why we have been chosen as the base for such an . . . indefinite establishment.'

Mary nodded in wonder, desperately trying to keep up with the diminutive officer's line of thought. Perhaps she was beginning to understand its craziness.

'It seems they would have us believe a line can no longer be drawn between Right and Wrong; that everything is just a Grey Area. We are the Grey Area, Mrs Carter . . .'

Mary's feeling of dread had increased to the point where she could barely think. The hundred and one questions piled into a log jam at the forefront of her brain, producing a debilitating anxiety, paralysing in its effect.

The smiling group captain uncapped his fountain pen and referred to his form. 'We have your name, your, ha-ha, real world address, your address here . . .'

He leaned forward in cheerful earnestness.

'I take it you have never killed anybody.'

'Killed? I can barely swat a fly!'

The smile gleamed as much as it could in the dull light. 'I don't think flies count, Mrs Carter — East Sector responsibility. Ever stolen anything?'

'No!'

The finger rose in debate. 'Many say "No" without thinking. Ever found anything and kept it without taking reasonable steps to trace the owner thereof?'

'No.'

'Ever accepted too much change in a shop? Kept anything you have mistakenly not paid for? Not paid back a debt?'

'I would never dream of such things!'

Her wide eyes and gaping mouth seemed to convince him. 'Now let me see . . .' He tapped his smiling monkey teeth with the fountain pen. 'Ever found another man attractive — that is to say, covet, or at least fantasised about?'

'Never! One removes oneself from the occasion of sin!'

The eyes smoothed out in warm relief behind the spectacles. 'Admirable, Mrs Carter! We have so very few, today. who can remember such simple advice in the avoidance of expensive complications, ha-ha . . .'

In fact, the station commander cheerfully continued with similar dilemma raising questions all the way to the bottom of his form.

'Ever taken the Lord's name in vain?'

This made her pause. 'I am guilty in small ways.'

Mary watched him ink in the relevant answer with his wobbling, scratching fountain pen. 'You're covering what Moses brought down from Mount Sinai, aren't you, sir?'

Smiling, Gabriel reversed the form and pressed it judiciously onto his blotter. 'We have to start somewhere, Mrs Carter. I've been trained to commence always with the basics.'

Mary fidgeted before the desk. 'People nowadays say life is too complicated.'

'Indeed it is, Mrs Carter. The Grey Area exists to undo the Gordian Knot of the affairs of modern man — and ladies, naturally, ha-ha.'

Mary gazed with her constant apprehension. 'It must take time, sir.'

The monkey smile became more fixed, as though a hard truth were shining through the officious manner. 'Here, we have a number of little pieces of theatre at our disposal, Mrs Carter. We can make things appear, or disappear. We can make people doubt the rather primitive and limiting laws of physics. What we cannot do is alter the actuality of things, as opposed to their illusion.'

The glowing little man settled deeper into his seat as he warmed to his theme.

'The Opposition can do the same, of course. He can take many forms, like the good Book says. He, too, can make water look and taste like wine — though it will remain water. We . . . cannot stop the march of Time. Time is the essence, Mrs Carter. We have our workload like any other organisation. For each case we are allocated twenty-four hours — no more, no less . . .'

More then ever, Mary felt afraid of the obsequious looking little man — so afraid, she was unable to blink in case something unimaginable manifested itself in the millisecond of darkness. 'What about my family, sir? Francis, Lucille, little Tommy . . .?'

The station commander brought all his relevant files together. He knocked them square on his desk. 'You are all classed as one, single case, Mrs Carter — even though every human being is as different as a falling raindrop. We call it Creative Accountancy. Our procedure is caused by the insidious pressure of caseload. My personal professional opinion is that you should not be here — not according to pure criteria. However . . . It means, you see, that you all collectively share the single allotted space of twenty-four hours.'

He pointed his fountain pen.

'That is a very nice Cartier replica Frank bought you for your anniversary, Mrs Carter. I advise you to check it.'

Mary was taken aback by his knowledge of something unknown outside the family and a couple of Frank's work mates. She peered at the square dial. 'Eleven o'clock.' Her voice was toneless.

Gabriel smiled. 'You, your husband and family, arrived in New Casterleck at six o'clock yesterday evening. You have seven hours left. There we have it.'

Mary stared. She looked out of the hut window at the wan daylight.

Gabriel's voice continued, smoothly, but with a hidden hard tone. 'I hope your battery is good, Mrs Carter. When your watch reads six o'clock, your collective time in Limbo is up . . .'

'What will happen then, sir?'

Gabriel spread his hands over the files. 'It will be time for you to leave the grey area of Limbo. Anyone still in custody will have to move on.'

With cold dread, Mary repeated his phrase. 'Move on . . .?'

'To whatever place and/or reward that is adjudged, be it good —' his eyes took on a hard light '— or bad . . .'

They remained either side of the big desk, official and civilian, static in the grey. Mary's question sounded hollow, as though uttered in a room that had been empty for years.

'What if they are not in custody?'

The officer suddenly found his animation, glowing smile spreading with what appeared to be intense innuendo. 'Then everything has to return to its starting point.'

'What does that mean, sir?'

'Every department, Mrs Carter, has its criterion, and procedures to fit. If resolution cannot be achieved within twenty-four hours, then Rejection has to be the automatic decision.'

'R-Rejection?'

'The application to move from Limbo will have been rejected. You therefore all have to return to the point of departure from your earthly existence until further data can be collated . . .'

There were three old Bakelite phones on the commander's desk: black, green, red. One of them rang. Gabriel raised a polite finger and picked up the green one. His smile fled.

'Do nothing until I get there.' His voice was sharp with authority. 'Please remain here, Mrs Carter. A slight problem.'

He left as a specialist in a fever hospital would. Seconds later, Mary heard voices in the corridor.

'Sergeant.'

'Sir!'

Brisk footsteps left the hut, outer door slamming.

Alone in the office, Mary became restless. She could hear sounds of parade ground drill. A voice screamed about Dressing.

'Look at you! Goring would piss his pants in the middle of France!'

Other shouts elsewhere were similar. 'Form up! Those things aren't broom handles!'

The bedlam going on about her masked the close, intimate sounds in the corridor. Mary turned her head — though in the midst of prayers to St Jude. Someone, distinctly non-military, was creeping down the corridor, A foot was sliding, as though its owner were injured. The door opened. Softly.

The horrific face, half bone, half flesh, brought Mary to the point of a scream.

'Ssh,' said the milkman softly. 'You must come with me. Now . . .'

***

Tommy cringed behind the blindfold, still tussling with his bonds. They'd said Ready. They'd said Aim.

Interminable seconds stretched, the rhythm of events broken.

He could hear a phone ringing.

The aero engine, far away, lost its high pitched song.

Pounding feet.

'Corporal of the guard!'

There was a buzz of discussion.

'Stand easy!'

The buzz grew to a rumble, then broke into a roar of disappointment from the huddle of ragged workmen. The roar collapsed into a hubbub of angry conversation, groans of frustration. The hum of a light vehicle drew near. Gears crashed, brakes squealed. Measured, crisp footsteps approached.

'Unload arms!'

***

Frank Carter slipped the old Atlantean up through the gears. He looked hard at his daughter.

'The hairdressers, eh?'

Lucy seemed her usual self, standing next to him on the platform. 'Why are you looking at me like that, Dad?'

'Just trying to figure what's different about you.'

Lucille lowered her head, hiding her hard, pale face behind the tumbling, brown curls.

'You've just proved my point, Lucy.'

'And what's that, Dad?'

'There's hardly been a peep out of you. Not a smile. What's happened to the girl who got herself expelled for noisy relationships with boys, eh?'

Still no sign of a smile. From behind the curls came a mutter. Inaudible.

'Say again, Lucy.'

'I said, I've left school.'

Frank watched the empty house shells spin by. The estate looked like a slowly revolving merry-go-round with no-one on it. 'Leaving school and moving house all in one movement . . .' he mused. 'We got very worried, you know. Nothing for you to do till things get established. No friends.' He jerked a thumb. 'Looks like we're the only residents in the whole place at the moment.'

The answer was hard. It was Lucy's voice all right, but without the bubble and squeak, as if a strange personality had moved in on her.

'But you went and did it anyway, didn't you?'

Frank frowned at the half hidden face. He could see a solitary eye burning through the curls. And that dress! It gave him the creeps.

'Don't you remember what you said, Lucy? "One thing I'm dead good at is making friends."' He sighed heavily, 'All my mates at the depot laughed, because they thought I didn't know . . .'

'Didn't know what, Dad?'

Frank shifted as though an army of ants were biting his legs. 'About you,' he whispered.

The bus droned on, empty except for the two of them. The backs of the half erected shops came into view. Frank pulled into the stop, engine idling.

'We've all got our weaknesses, Lucy. They make us what we are.'

The hard voice cut from within the brown veil of curls. 'That's today's pearl of wisdom, is it?'

Frank was too surprised to be angry. 'What's got into you, then? Or shouldn't I ask?'

Lucy stepped off the platform, lightly, but gracefully. No juvenile bounce at all. 'I told you, I've left school.'

Puzzled and sad, Frank tried his panto villain laugh. It always raised a smile from her. Not this time. Lucille Carter just turned her cold face away, strode across the road toward the back of the shops.

Curiously adult.

***

Matt Ryland nodded with decision. 'We go on, Keith. They have no choice but to fund us, and I shall be reminding them of such if I have to.'

They were poking around the wreckage of the site. Keith found the wall plan from the cabin, strangely intact, only ripped at the corners where it had been torn from the wall. The Company Range Rover was lying on its side. The two of them righted it and found the engine started OK. Odd. Not even a dent.

They spread the wall plan on the bonnet. Ryland stabbed with his cheroot. 'We'll use that show house on the end, OK?'

Keith nodded.

'I'll complete my inspection, Keith — get a rough idea of the scale of the damage. You wait for the gang and show 'em the house, OK?'

'Right you are, Mr Ryland. I'll just stick to my original work allocations; reorganise when we find out what the frigging wind did.'

'Gotcha!' said Ryland with a fierce grin. Briskly, he strode away.

Keith shook his head at his boss's retreating back.

Rummaging around some more, he found the kettle and most of the mugs. Provisions were still intact in the disembodied cupboard. Nothing had been split or broken. Weird.

'I say!'

Bare metres away was a broken figure in a leather bomber jacket. Half its face had been scraped away, the other half was black with soot. Oddly, the hair was immaculate, parted in the centre.

The figure lurched forward sickeningly, voice an unearthly wheeze.

'*I want your life.*'

***

400 metres away on the far side of the proposed school was the part completed row of shops.

They were the only retail outlets planned for the New Casterleck overspill and their frontages yawned breeze blocks like empty mouths. No fittings or furnishings, not even the names of businesses or galvanised shutters brought any individuality to the shells.

A gentle wind had got up. It lifted the tumbling brown curls from Lucille's face. She could see two men far away on the dusty site, one with a white hat. The other looked odd.

About the same distance away, between the houses, she saw the man in the suit and the green wellingtons walking through, white hat bobbing.

None of them interested her, though she recognised the man in the suit. Her lip curled as she looked away.

It was the barren row of shops that took her attention. She stared at them with growing power and concentration, lips compressing in what seemed like more of the hate that drove her.

The second shop from the right.

The air about it began to shimmer. It could have been a master shot in a movie: an insert taking on its own independent life in a different time. Shapes solidified within. Mirrors. Sinks. Chairs. The sedentary hair dryers. Assistants — living.

Other images crossed the front display window that had melted in with a ripple of light waves. They came from nothing, vibrated to nothing when they'd passed by.

Not only that.

Within the narrow field of the shop, day turned to night, lights burning into the blue twilight, then darkness, rain and shine, and back to morning . . .

When one of the chairs was unoccupied, Lucille Carter entered the hairdressers.

'Hi, Lucy. What are you this week?'

'A blonde rinse, please.'

***

'**This** way, Mary.' The milkman pushed her across the mud between the huts with his cold gauntlets. 'It's all sorted out. You're only here for a short stay.' He shrugged, scratching rotting tissue beneath his helmet. 'Something to do with impure thoughts. Hmph. Hard to believe.'

Suddenly, he dragged her behind one of the ramshackle huts — a long one. Mary frowned. Inside, a woman was packing a parachute, the skeins of silk stretched along a line of rough trestle tables.

That couldn't have been spooking the abomination, thought Mary. Across the top of the mud street, two SPs walked, white batons swinging.

'The curse of the monkeys!' wheezed the milkman.

'What?'

But he was dragging her again. 'We must hurry. If anything goes wrong, you'll be stuck here with the rest of us in the Paradise of Fools!'

'Who's "us"?'

He was shepherding her towards the huge hangar. 'The prisoners of Limbo!' he croaked, as though it were a universal fact.

Mary began to resist, to pull back. 'My husband! My children!'

The milkman's gauntlet crushed like ice. 'Till death do us part, remember? Now come on, child. I've signed out the Rapide. You're free!'

In the cool darkness of the hangar, grey arc lamps were jury rigged over disembodied Merlin engines hoisted onto stout wooden trestles. Beyond the far door, out in the open, was a stripped Lancaster, wheeled scaffolding pushed under its naked wings.

'103 foot wingspan, see?' grinned the milkman. 'The standard hangar's only a 100.'

Close to the far wall was an ancient, twin engined biplane. It had stylish lines, but looked very frail.

A curio.

Mary was escorted past the engines and the scattered cowlings. Men looked, then looked away. There was a general air of conspiracy. She was bundled into the passenger cabin. It had wicker seats. Quaint.

The milkman had stumbled through and was climbing into the cabin next to the pilot — a pale, skeletal form. The pilot turned his head and croaked, 'Two six!' out of the sliding Perspex panel in the window. With a chuffing sound, the port prop whirled into a blur. When both props were turning, the pilot wheezed, 'Mag drop OK!'

Below, an erk unplugged a trolley acc and tugged it away.

'Chocks away!'

Large wedges were kicked and hauled away on hemp ropes.

The tiny aircraft taxied out of the cathedral-like hangar. Tearfully praying, Mary pressed her face against the vibrating Perspex. The ten tenths cloud had begun to move. It looked like the inside of a boiling kettle, swirling, twisting, to reveal a rotating tunnel that led up, up, out of the world, to an ethereal light that beckoned with a promise brighter than gold.

Mary's face softened into awe as she saw the fluffy white clouds gather like the robes of a spirit greater than herself, or any mortal conception, that radiated the euphoria she felt, plus the waves of relief that followed the anxiety of living.

Colour.

It invaded the aircraft with shafts of pure gold.

Mary's father turned in his seat, his smile young beneath his neatly parted hair. 'We'll soon get you where you belong, Mary, my child,' he said. 'Want us to overfly where your van pranged? The crash crews get a good laugh at the way they faff around these days.'

The uplifting feeling of the golden moment, the wish fulfilment, made Mary clasp her hands in thanksgiving.

There was only one false note.

As she gazed in wonder up the swirling tunnel to the light, a single, plaintive voice called across her fading, earthly memory.

Mum! Mummy! Please help me. They're going to shoot me. I've never ever never ever been so deep in the shit!

The old Rapide was turning off the peri-track onto the slip road that led to the secondary runway. The pilot had coarsened the pitch to slow forward speed — until someone leaned over the roof of the control tower to fire a green Very.

Mary, eyes wide, grasped the wicker back of the seat in front.

'Wait!'

Dad twisted in his seat. His face was stark with horror. Colour was draining from his complexion. 'No!' he cried. 'Even the CO has turned a blind eye!'

But Mary was at the cabin door tugging at the handle.

Mummmmeeee! screamed the voice in her head.

'Mary!' cried Dad from the cabin.

Everything was greying out. The features of her father and the pilot were suppurating to their previous state of frozen decay.

The cabin door swung open. Grass flowed by next to the peri track.

'Mary! Child! Please! Your immortal s —'

Mary jumped.

***

'**Release** the boy,' said the group captain.

'Sir!'

The corporal waved a bitterly aloof, but disciplined hand. Two of the erks stumbled to remove Tommy's blindfold.

The grey light was not powerful enough to blind him for long, and Tommy could see Mum running between the huts beyond the sandbags. A moment later, they untied him from the post and he was sobbing in her arms.

'I know it's only a dream, Mum, but it's so real! The bastards were going to shoot me!'

Mary watched his face brighten. Behind her, the group captain was talking to the corporal before the wrath filled gaze of the sergeant of the guard.

'I hate to countermand orders already given by any of my men, Corporal, but I have to say you were beyond the pale!'

The corporal was At Attention. 'War Emergency Rules, sir,' he intoned.

'Those rules only apply in strict battle conditions, Corporal. To be precise, on the actual field of battle.'

'Sir.'

The sergeant, pace stick clamped beneath stiff arm, took a pace forward to add his own comment in full parade ground voice. 'In other words, Corporal, you are in the shit!'

'Sergeant.'

The group captain raised a finger. 'Oh, there'll be no official charge, Sergeant. In different circumstances he would probably be commended for his initiative. We are at war after all.'

Both sergeant and corporal chorused as one: 'Sir!'

Tommy was still in Mary's shocked arms. He began to shake with laughter. 'What a pair of assholes!'

'Thomas!' As group captain, sergeant and corporal turned to look, Mary admonished him. 'You are very naughty, Thomas. You must show respect to your elders.'

'You gotta be kidding, right?'

Before the tense atmosphere could be broken, a wailing siren split the grey. All turned to look at the control tower. A man in a flat tin hat and gas mask satchel was turning a handle for all he was worth on the roof of the tower.

'Hey!' said Tommy, wriggling from his mother's grasp.

Someone else on the roof fired a red Very light at the wide expanse of tarmac. There was the growing whine of high pitched aero engines on full boost. From beyond the tarmac runway, a tiny aircraft was hurtling in toward them. Another, even lower, was in its wake. Flashes of the lightest grey sparkled along both sets of wings.

'Messerschmidts!' cried Tommy.

Several columns of spitting earth commenced a deadly march toward the watching personnel. Men ran in all directions. Several whistles blew.

'Battle conditions,' muttered the corporal bitterly.

'The effrontery!' exclaimed the group captain.

The sergeant grabbed Mary and Tommy and hurled them into a slit trench then jumped in after them, in single flowing action. 'We are under attack!' he informed them.

'No shit, Sherlock!' said Tommy.

Another figure landed in the trench. The group captain straightened the braided peak of his cap, smiling apology. 'The hun has no consideration, unfortunately.'

As the exploding fountains of earth swept by, the sergeant blew his whistle. 'Man the Lewis guns!' he roared.

The corporal ran to gather men. The group captain and the sergeant left the trench.

Mary grasped Tommy. 'Come at once!'

They darted between the huts, Mary steering the boy toward the main gate . . .

White Hat turned his hard face. His teeth bared when he was unable to spot the boy. He began to lead his work force toward the main gate, ignoring the flap, the running erks, the circling and screaming Messerschmidts. The yellow hardhats of the workmen bobbed raggedly as they passed the slit trenches, all out of step.

The sergeant went into paroxysms of fury. 'Get under cover, you sodding shower!'

The limping man with the squeaking side cutters threw out a single, obscene finger. 'Bugger off, Sergeant.'

The group captain tried to explain. 'They are outside our jurisdiction, Sergeant.'

'You!' White Hat was pointing at the group captain, teeth bared. 'You're no more a judge than my ass!'

***

Frank Carter drove the Atlantean through each of the villages printed on his running board. As the stated times seemed laid down for coach and horses, he had to stand down for several minutes in each.

Grey people boarded and alighted. Frank was reminded of children's TV: Trumpton. There was the postman, the baker, the butcher, the policeman — all on their way to their trades. All said Good Morning and remarked on the weather, the harvest prospects, hold-ups at market, certain drunken and shady local characters.

They smiled with their mouths, but not their eyes.

The route was a circular one, rarely venturing close to civilisation, which remained hidden beyond the all pervading grey mist. The only passenger Frank felt affinity with was one of the drunks the policeman had referred to. He got on near a lonely police lockup on the edge of the moor, slumping onto the platform smelling of the previous night's celebrations.

'I got no money, but I'll sing ye a song!'

Naturally, he serenaded the passengers all the way back to Old Casterleck where they all got off in front of The Hanging Ditch.

Frank ran up to Mangle Street Depot empty.

Monkey climbing the old bus round the tight corner, he was relieved to see someone standing in the double doorway. The squat little man was wearing blue serge and the old style blue peaked cap of a depot inspector. As his pale face bore an indulgent grin, Frank opened the narrow entrance door preparing to stop.

The inspector waved his hand, directing him round the side to the rear yard.

Frank Carter backed up in the yard, then walked through with his Almex and cash bag. Most of the other buses were out.

The inspector joined him in the conductors' room. 'I thought it were thee,' he said, puffing on his pipe. 'A lot of transferees would have waited for someone to show up.'

Frank nodded. 'Did I do right, then? Wasn't sure.'

The inspector pointed his pipe. 'It's all on the notices, young man. Surprising how so many of today's lot have to make simple things complicated.'

Frank expelled air with relief. 'It's an isolated spot, Inspector.'

'That it be.'

'I just had visions of people being stuck if I didn't get going.'

'That's the spirit!' The inspector nodded. 'Visions . . .' he mused.

Something about the way the grey faced little man grinned up at him made Frank nervous. 'Shall I carry on with the spare Almex?'

The inspector grinned away, nodding, as if Frank had never spoken.

'Just wondered if you had the Wayfarer thing with the computer system.'

'Good heavens no! This job's complicated enough. You've done the first part of your split, young man. You toddle off home for some nose bag; back here for —' consulting the wall clock, which was correct '—1700, yes? Thank ee very much, young man.'

Frank was left alone with the large old clock whose fingers denoted 1140. At least they were using the modern twenty-four hour system.

The self-drive was still in the corner of the yard where he'd parked it. Frank climbed in and turned the key.

The engine fired.

***

'I don't wanna go home, Mum,' whined Tommy. 'I wanna stay and watch the aeroplanes. Are they making a movie?'

Mary hung onto his hand like grim death — mentally changing the simile with a silent Act of Contrition. 'Your father will be home shortly. He's on a split.'

'He won't do owt,' scoffed Tommy.

'We need to have a talk, Tommy.'

'Haven't done owt.'

'It's not about what you did, or didn't do.'

'Hey, does this mean I'm not in the shit, then?'

Mary fumbled in her purse for the door key, shaking her scarf-wrapped head in despair. 'We've just moved house, Tommy. A line has been drawn. We must start afresh. It's our only hope, dear Lord.'

Tommy thrust his hands in his pockets on the garden cinders. 'I get it — we've all got to be good.'

'Yes!' Mary got the front door open at last and hustled Tommy inside whilst peering anxiously up and down the grey ring road.

'Boring!' said Tommy.

No sooner had Mary slammed the door to on the flimsy Yale-type lock, than someone knocked. Mary froze. Tommy was in the kitchen already, hanging over the sink to look through the window.

'Get down!' she hissed.

'It's our Lucy. Hey!'

Gasping with relief, Mary opened the door. She recoiled from the blonde, slim, alien figure.

'By all the saints, Lucille! What have you done?'

***

Frank fastened his seat belt, put the Transit into first.

The appearance of the figure in the passenger seat made him stall the engine in his shock. Perhaps the man had been sitting there all the time. There was nothing about him of the all enveloping grey that deadened the people and the surroundings of the neighbourhood.

The hair of the figure was shoulder length. Golden. The piercing eyes, blue. Even the flesh had a translucence that glowed with its own luminosity in the deepest shadow.

How could he have not seen him?

Frank jolted in his seat. Adrenalin surged through his arterial and nervous systems, sparking over into his musculature, urging him to flight.

The golden man said nothing, merely turning to him with his glowing eyes. No words were spoken, or needed to be spoken. Their minds just met.

A golden hand — the right one — settled on Frank's shoulder.

Frank became rigid, as though touched by a bolt of ethereal energy.

SIX

ALL kinds of ideas and images poured into Frank Carter's brain as he sat behind the wheel of the self-drive Transit next to the Golden Being. They came from the burning blue eyes, even the flaming hair.

He could see the myriad of pointless existences of mortal men: wars, idiocies, words, behaviour, philosophies. They seemed secondary, trite, when compared to the limitless sweep of eternity.

Protect

Money, entertainment, relief from anxieties of all kinds: They seemed to pale into the same grubbiness as the grey that surrounded this lesser perfection.

Your

Even if the Being with the golden hair could hurt him with his touch, it wouldn't have mattered in the overall scheme of real existence.

Immortal

The golden right hand remained on Frank Carter's shoulder, immobilising him. Spirit and knowledge connected between them like great, natural force as Frank gaped open-mouthed in inferior, mortal shock as the blue eyes burned from the godlike features.

S o u l

The other golden hand, the left, reached slowly toward him in the shabby little van; reached across until it all but touched Frank's perspiring forehead.

It moved slowly as though its movement were taking place in a different, superior dimension. The left fingers moved down from his forehead to his navel, then across, from shoulder to shoulder.

A genuflection.

He'd seen Mary do it often enough.

Then: a final thought. A concept. Again it was without earthly communication.

Go in peace.

And:

Blessed be.

The god, or prophet, dematerialised as suddenly as it had come. Frank was left alone, twisting and turning his head in as many directions as possible, casting electric, frenetic glances. Meanwhile, the van's engine restarted. All by itself.

Against the drab grey surroundings appeared the shambling figure of the drunken rustic who'd been on Frank's back all the way into Old Casterleck. Grinning, he sprawled against the Triplex safety glass of the windscreen with a thump, mouth forming cheerful and dribbling inanities within the swarthy grey of his complexion.

'Shall I sing thee a song? I want your life!'

***

Lucille swept into the little pebble-dash house. Her golden curtain of hair dazzled.

Tommy sniggered. Mary stared.

Mary was used to Lucille slinking around, arms folded, head bowed, face half hidden by the chestnut curls. The silly girl was always sliding glances from the side of her eyes, constantly expecting interrogation, admonishment.

Except when boys were around.

Then there was the up-from-under-look, and the grin of sly promise and challenge; a posture of giving and offering what she should not, shoulders back, chest thrust out, God save her — all the wrong signals of inherent weakness that were so worrying.

Until now.

Lucille swept into the kitchen and said, 'I've gone blonde, OK?'

As Mary remained speechless and sad, Tommy said, 'Hey, if she can't do it now, when can she do it? Jesus H!'

A vocalisation was finally wrung from her. 'Thomas!'

'Shit, I forgot.'

But the girl gazed back at her mother, hand in hip. An equal.

'Where did you get that striped dress from, Lucille?'

'I've had it ages, Mum.'

'It's cool!' said Tommy. 'Clings in all the right places, kid!'

Mary was confused, wringing her hands, memory uncertain before the glare of sheer personality now confronting her. 'You look like someone else . . .'

'Huh,' said Tommy. ''Bout time.'

Which made Lucille turn her gaze upon him.

Mary watched, looking for the secret messages she knew passed between brother and sister. Normally, the boy stared back fifty for one. This time, he broke eye contact first, evoking a silence that made Mary uncomfortable.

She decided, for once, to back-pedal. 'You certainly look different.'

'Colour,' said Tommy, unexpectedly. As mother and daughter looked at him, he scratched his groin awkwardly, searching for words.

'She's in colour. . .'

It was true! Mary felt goose pimples cover her flesh like bacteria as the realisation sank in. Other things seeped through to her left brain, powered by the intuitive superstition of her right brain.

'The shops,' said Mary, weakly.

'What about 'em?'

A hard glint in Lucille's eyes made Mary stammer and wring her hands all the more. 'Th-they're built, then?'

Lucille shrugged. 'I got what I wanted.'

Mary stared, fearing the evasiveness she detected in the girl's answer.

'Look, Mum, you've had a big day. You're stressed out. Go and lie down till Dad gets back. OK?'

Watched by her children, Mary broke eye contact and retreated to the stairs, uncomfortable because she could detect manoeuvring — adolescent manipulation with its mandatory straying from the path of . . .

'Rest, Mum. Take five.'

The stairs creaked beneath as she retired from the powerhouse presence emanating from the charismatic blue eyes and the flesh coloured flesh.

Colour.

As Tommy said, real and live in a grey world.

Where had it come from?

***

Tommy Carter gazed in awe at his new-look sister. She was standing right there in the kitchen, adult yet approachable and . . . Great!

'Hey, ya've really got this lot sussed, ain't ya?'

A thin smile played at Lucy's mouth. Yet the eyes stayed cool and blue and all-knowing. 'Yes, Tommy. You could say that.' Tommy was about to gush again, but Lucy said, 'Brew up, will you?'

'Yeah!'

The kettle was filled and on the New World before Tommy realised what was happening. She'd given him an order, and he was obeying.

Lucy folded her arms and moved gracefully into the dinette. She stared at the back door with its frosted glass panel. The blue eyes glowed. She rubbed her talons together in little circles, palms horizontal.

Rubbed and rubbed.

Until she felt the gathering power . . .

A shape. Indistinct at first, it moved on the cinder path at the back of the house. It remained distorted by the bubbles in the glass.

***

Mary carefully shut the door to the master bedroom behind her.

She'd been tempted to peek into Lucille's bedroom, intuition and right brain telling her it contained some clue. But a power prevented her. She'd even stopped wringing her hands long enough to place one palm on the aluminium handle. Somehow, her daughter's room had stayed solidly shut.

Taboo.

She found lying on her own bed difficult, even on top of the soft duvet. There was the sin of Sloth, and the Christian Work ethic, acting like invisible nails in her psyche. Night was for resting. But the force of the Personality dulled her instincts and resistance and drew her into the soft bosom of the duvet.

The Order. Take five . . .

The spinning sensation convinced her she was doing the right thing. Spinning. It actually took shape above her head: a whirling, inverted cone; a vortex that drew her almost physically, lifting weight from her while shrinking her vigilance.

Vigilance.

An old, uncompromising word. Its appearance in the whirl of her consciousness made her more physically aware. The floating sensation of being lifted up into the vortex became more like solid flight. She even bumped gently against the ceiling — which immediately softened into a blancmange-like substance.

Shaped

Into the false features of a Super Being from a forbidden dimension.

Forbidden. Another hard word of the World.

It made her feel she should not be looking into such a face, even though its features moulded warmly into a welcoming smile.

There was a hint . . . Fangs, rather than teeth . . . The glinting eyes of a beast.

The Beast.

A quick glance over her shoulder revealed the mechanics of it all. Her physical being remained on the bed, natural, arms enfolded across her chest in the sleep of the righteous, as Father used to say.

All while the ceiling smiled its dubious smile.

C o m e . . .

***

Matt Ryland paced purposefully along the cinder paths between the house units.

His frown increased. He should have reached the track of storm devastation by now. They'd seen it; seen the way units on the edge of it had been ripped in half, as if by a child tired of its toys. You could even see the broken rafters poking against the damn grey of the sky for Christ' sake!

It was when he had to pass in front of a windowless but intact row of units, through a strange ripple of air rather like that caused by the warm outflow of a giant heating duct, and . . .

Well, all the units were intact.

Exasperated, Ryland looked in every direction at once, like a dupe in a children's cartoon. All about him — perfect, intact units.

No sign of storm damage whatsoever . . .

OK. Ryland retraced his steps to the flow of hot air that had made everything shimmer and change. No sign of that either. His white hardhat cocked this way and that as he scanned the windows. The area looked familiar.

Fondly familiar.

Just round this corner. Yeah! There was the cinder path that led past the only occupied house he'd seen. Taking it, he looked up at the window where he'd seen the young girl preening herself. Hot pants — wow! There'd been a blonde as well — the chick in the striped dress.

On the ground floor of this house he fancied he saw movement behind the frosted glass panel of the back door. Imagination, probably. Freudian imagination.

Speculatively, he tapped his clipboard on his knuckles.

Which was when he saw the dark haired woman.

***

The smile of the ceiling became more convivial. Was it really the workings of Mary's tired imagination? It seemed so real.

A grand, old man . . .

He was smiling down upon her, comfortably inhabiting the new distemper-sealed plaster as if he had a divine right to be there. He had rosy cheeks and billowing white clouds for a beard and gentle father's eyes. Soothing. It seemed he actually breathed out a sigh.

Mary's last, fearful glance revealed the luminous, silken cord that grew from the third eye claimed by the mystics to be normally invisible on her physical body (which wasn't, couldn't, be real, anyway). Floating almost hypnotically, Mary allowed herself to be drawn up and into the ceiling . . . Everything was still grey. Real? Perhaps all of this New Casterleck place was a dream.

She was standing by the window, arms folded. She felt well, alive, vital. But strung up. Some inner torment churned within her. Yet she'd not been transported to some feared place. She was simply looking through the window of her master bedroom.

She even looked at the bed. The duvet was hollowed, but empty.

She was thinking of Francis — Frank, to everyone else. He would be here soon. She could even remember that. He might feel the same restlessness. He'd paw her coyly, make silly jokes in his mock US voice. He would go quite far — but not far enough.

Such thoughts of the physical made her bosom swell, trapped as it was, demurely, within her folded arms.

Something made her straighten herself out, press her shoulders back. She could now feel the thrust of her hardening nipples against the material of her bra and dress. Her right hand toyed with a lock of her own hair.

Hair.

From the side of her eye, it looked distinctly black: none of the pepper and salt that had appeared with the gentle press of the years. And her skin. It felt creamy. Wrinkle free. She wasn't young, but she wasn't old. At the peak. . . The tingling spread from her breasts to her abdomen, down to the neglected and forbidden zone of the thighs, buttocks, pubic arch.

There was a Presence.

But it was out in the Grey of the drab surroundings of partially built future households. She couldn't see any physical manifestation of it, but sensed a whimsical amusement from some huge, watchful Being. Encouragement.

E n j o y.

A man was standing on the cinder path at the back of the house. He was about the same age as Mary herself, well proportioned, immaculate in suit, white hardhat, green wellingtons. He had to be one of the construction officials.

He gestured to her, smiling.

Before she could stop, she smiled back. In welcome. She raised a creamy arm in acknowledgement. With grace.

Mary opened the bedroom door. 'Lucille? Thomas?'

No answer.

Anxiety formed at the outer edge of her mind. But it was pushed away quite easily by the Presence, like the dust of existence being swept under the carpet — something the Real Mary would never do. The old man in the ceiling smiled his unseen encouragement. She felt the whole Existentialist philosophy of living for the Here and Now sweep up into a single, everyday, innocuous phrase.

Be a devil . . .

Odd that the stairs did not creak. She certainly felt as though she were walking on air, gracefully, enjoying the sensual feel of her Spirit, her creamy flesh against her clothes.

The building official smiled down at her as she opened the back door. Funny how she just could not stand demurely, her usual self, arms tightly folded as though in respectful subservience. Instead, she placed an arm on the door jamb, shoulders back, armpit exposed. Flaunting, thrusting. Easy!

And he . . .

There was no Grey in his features, either. His teeth were white, eyes sparkling blue. She could actually see the colour rise to his cheeks; hear his involuntary flustering as he spoke.

'I, ha, wonder if you've experienced any freak weather conditions, Madam. Storm damage? By the way, sorry, I'm from the Housing Department.'

And she . . .

The old Mary would have answered his questions: nervously, deferentially, primly, briefly.

'Well, I doubt you're a serial rapist. I don't have that sort of luck. Come in for a tea. Don't kid me that's not what you really want.'

Simple, slick, oblique dialogue that would, should, never have entered her head.

It's not real, said the Being in the ceiling.

The New Mary stepped back just enough to let him by her, his knuckles just brushing the lower swell of her breast.

It doesn't count.

Then closed the door behind him, leaned round him, up-from-under, never breaking eye contact or letting the half smile slip; making him feel masculine and superior, the way they had to feel, aware that the top of her dark, sleek head only came to the jib of his chin. Yeah!

Mary watched herself wiggle into the kitchen in front of him with the jelly chassis she'd seen others flaunt with disapproval.

Doesn't count.

Odd. The kettle was just coming to the boil. Mugs stood ready on the work surface, tea bags ready. Must have been the children before they'd slid off.

And her voice. The things she was saying!

'Hungry as well, I suppose. Aren't we all? As regards storms and damage — nothing happens round here. No-one's tried to damage me in yonks. How about you?'

The official was sitting on Frank's stool, so that the positions were falsely reversed, his head being level with her delicate chin. The New Mary put a steaming mug near him, letting her fingers stray to his shoulder as he said, 'Who would want to damage you, my love?'

'It's a pretend thing, really. Role playing. It's exciting to think a man could violate you, if he wanted to. Mm . . .?'

She watched the New Mary take the clipboard from his grasp, lay it next to the mug, take the big, well kept hands, place them on her tingling breasts. The New voice shocked her, the way it whispered like a demon.

'Cream cake sex, yeah? Not as lavish as a home cooked meal, but they can be over facing — all the time. Mm . . .? No need to worry about how I'd spend your money, or what I drink, or what my taste in books, films, CDs is. No need to talk at all, or have consideration for anything but the moment, yeah?'

Above all, Mary wondered where the words were coming from. Certainly she'd heard of girls who lured men this way. The words were spoken in her own voice, too. She could recognise it as incontrovertibly hers.

Was it all coming from her?

A hidden place she dared not confess to?

And there was the pleasure that radiated from the well kept hands that roved over her, pulled her toward the powerful, protective triangle of the strange man's physique. The dress was being slipped from her shoulders; the bra being carefully unhooked.

And that most private place that was always kept so hidden from anyone who could possibly see it — even in the showers at school decades ago; the downy hair that hid the lips that enclosed the red satin. All was being carefully investigated and examined with growing, mutual excitement . . .

'No!'

Still her voice, but different. Hard, Cold. Actual. Grey . . .

The ceiling. The features she imagined within it hardened too. There was a scowl of disappointment. Rage. The glint of teeth.

Mary was lying in bed still on top of the duvet. The air outside was grey, drab, insubstantial. Her eyes, having sprung open, flitted from side to side in her head. The ceiling had hardened back to fresh plaster with its newly applied distemper, a flat paint that bore no marks or ripples that could be manufactured by earthly imagination into anything other than a plain surface.

Voices.

'You can't, Tommy. Mum said . . .'

Stifled giggles. The click of a door catch.

When Mary heard the engine of the self-drive van, she knew she was back in concrete reality. Except for certain details.

Her patina of sweat.

Her dress, pulled down to her waist.

Her bra dangled from the windowsill.

It looked as though it had been carelessly, wantonly discarded, thrown there by an eager, fantasy lover, the touch of whose well kept hands still lingered, even though no-one was there. The window was ajar, curtains lifting and falling like caressing limbs.

The marks on her bosom. They followed the shape and furrows of grasping fingers . . .

***

Frank Carter was still in a daze of turmoil. Disarray. He walked up the cinders of the path. At the front door, he fumbled for his key.

From inside the house he heard light footsteps rumble and creak down the stairs. When the door was flung open, he flinched.

'Mary?'

He stared at her flushed cheeks. The top buttons of her dress were undone. He could feel his eyeballs flicking from detail to unfamiliar detail. Odd. Awry. Not right.

He swallowed. 'You look as though someone's given you a turn.'

Suddenly, he felt afraid of her. It didn't seem possible. It was the way she tugged him through the doorway, grasping his hand in both of hers.

'What —'

She collapsed against him, cheeks wet, bosom heaving. Idiot data flowed in from his right brain. Images. Some blonde beast from the id who'd tear her out of his arms with the superior strength of a Being from. . .

'You're all out of breath, Mary!'

He led her into the kitchen, relieved that her wild strength had receded. Despite his sudden, unreasonable terror, Frank was unable to help peering down at the fold of flesh where her neck joined her shoulder. And the dress. She seemed to be bulging out of it. He slid his free hand down to cover the curve of her buttocks.

Unable to prevent his sudden, urgent need, he pressed himself against her.

Their eyes met for an unholy second.

But the heat went. She made the familiar gestures, shaking her head, her hand. 'Please, Frank.'

Lifting his head, Frank saw a familiar shape in the dinette. The female form was outlined in grey, wearing the striped dress that still surfaced in his nightmares.

Only it was upright, now, and moving.

Frank froze, eyes feeling they were protruding onto his cold cheeks. The shape passed through onto the kitchen, its shadow falling away.

Lucy.

And yet . . .

The face was Lucy's. Yet it wasn't. No sign of the gap-toothed grin, and the eyes were hard. Accusing. As though he'd been caught up with for some guilty act.

His erection, of course, collapsed.

'Hi, Dad.'

The three of them remained frozen in tableau in the grey kitchen. Until Mary got them seated at the gate-leg table in the dinette in her quietly authoritative way. Frank scratched his head in unbearable, unreasonable frustration. Amazing how Mary could exude authority and deference all at the same time. By now, she'd fastened her buttons all the way up to the top, the way she did winter and summer, making sure her crucifix was visible on the outside of the material. Frank wanted to tear it from her, a voice raging in his head:

Why does she not lapse?

Silly.

The crucifix had always been there, part of her, like the picture of the pope and the Sacred Heart icon and the picture of her dad and his crew. Take 'em or leave 'em. Honour thy father and thy mother. No New English Bible translation for her.

The way they sat at the table seemed so typical too: Mary on one side, Frank and Lucy like errant children on the other.

'We must talk about this place. First, where's Tommy?'

Lucy shrugged. 'Said he'd be back when Dad got home.'

'I told you that neither of you were to float off before we talked.'

Again, the shrug. 'You know what he's like, Mum.'

Frank stared. Lucy seemed to be playing the part of . . . Lucy. Even the juvenile shrug seemed forced. And the blue eyes. They burned with hate.

Mary wrung her hands as she prepared to address them, as though she felt her family were about to be torn from her. Her insecure actions made the crucifix dance on its chain, sending pale butterflies into the greys of ever gathering shadow.

One flickered on Lucy's cheek.

Unwinking, she swatted it like a fly.

'This place,' said Mary, 'is not what it seems.'

Lucy. Her lip was curling into a smile. Not one of her specials, something darker. Her lips parted, as though about to emit something hurtful. Faith shaking.

Frank jumped in. 'You can say that again! There's some right weird characters around, straight out of the ark. I reckon they all sealed themselves into a time warp to escape the Great Plague!'

Tentatively at first, they began to swap stories. Mary and Frank. Lucy did not speak.

***

Tommy walked head down along the ring road, hands in pockets.

The grey emptiness narked him now. He imagined the road surfaced with the familiar tarmac, glinting with stabbing shards of sunlight glancing off windscreens and chrome strip.

The smell.

The loved smell of exhaust gas and spent fuel and melting tar . . .

The air. It shimmered like it did on hot summer days in the school hols when clothes stuck to the skin.

The noise.

The engine noise had just arrived. Not with a start. Couldn't have. It had obviously built from some distance away, unnoticed. The actual appearance of the black car on the unmade ring road was the same: appearing, slowing, gliding up beside Tommy like a big, black cat, engine purring on tick over.

Tommy gaped.

It wasn't a fancy set of wheels — just the old, black Capri of his yearning memory, its long, sleek bonnet still hand rollered in black cellulose. Tommy dared not move or breathe. It was a dream, easily shattered by boring reality, the dearth of wish fulfilment. Odd, within the dull grey that depressingly overlaid the New Casterleck estate, the car appeared to have its own halo of sunlight. Even its windows reflected its own supply of colour.

The hairs were well risen on the nape of Tommy's neck as the side window lowered sedately. Tommy's mouth fell open.

The private sunlight revealed the right hand on the steering wheel. Right there, on the third finger, was the pewter dress ring in the shape of a skull — dated, naff, yet real.

'Rick?'

The driver's face remained hidden in the shadow of black, greased hair — real shadow, cast by strong sunlight, rather than the wishy-washy grey that deadened everything so. There was also the smell of something rotting, sort of creeping out of the lowered side window.

The voice from inside the car sounded breathy, wheezy, croaky, damaged beyond repair.

'Tommy! There you go!'

Tommy felt cold. Slightly queasy. Rick was dressed in his usual black leathers. It was just like he'd decided to drop out for six months, then get deposited back in the World exactly as he'd left it. Rick's Law, yeah? Oh boy!

'They said you were dead, Rick!'

The damaged voice sounded far away. 'Rumours, man. Rick cannot be killed.'

Tommy felt his smile spreading as the nasty, cold feeling warmed away. His heart felt lighter as the car's sunlight halo flickered about him.

'But it was in the paper, Rick. The car — this car — spun in a four wheel slide of death right under the braking tanker. The driver's head was sheared. Richard Donald, known as Rick, twenty-five year old resident of . . . Straight up, man!'

'Anything else, dude?'

'Yeah! Your head . . . It was never found.'

The shadowy face remained in silhouette, just the glint of widely exposed teeth speckling the shadow. 'Rumours, man. Rumours . . .'

'But —'

'This car, yeah?'

'It was this car, Rick. Same reg. Your car!'

The hand with the skull ring drummed the steering wheel. 'Take a look see. Any ripples in the body, man? Any different shade of black?'

Mouth still hanging in awe, Tommy squatted to examine the smooth lines of the wing, the sill, the bonnet that went on and on.

The boy even ran respectful fingers along the surfaces, seeking out joins and overlays his eyes could not find.

The wheeze snickered. 'Some things are above the mortal plane, dude. They have the luck of the Devil, y'might say. Heh!'

'Yeah!' Tommy rose to his feet, smile practically touching his ears.

'Now why doncha just forget yore earthly cares, man? Just for a little while. It's what ya have to do when ya ride with Rick.'

In added invitation, the nearside door, now roadside, clicked open, yawning like a secret tomb.

'Do ya mean it, Rick?'

'Rick does not kid over wheels, man.'

Tommy moved to the front of the car, then paused. His face fell. 'I, uh, promised Mum . . .' But something about the shadow behind the glistening windscreen, lancing sun, made his protest die.

'Earthly cares, man,' wheezed Rick.

It was enough. Tommy skipped round the old black Capri in its bubble of sun, got into the passenger bucket seat, sank willingly into the upholstery. Excited, he looked across at Rick.

The wide rows of teeth sparkled in the shadow. A dated Chelsea boot tramped the gas pedal. The grey house shells flew into a blur as Tommy was pressed into the seat back.

'Where we going, man?'

'When you ride with Rick,' wheezed the damaged voice box, 'it's only the feeling that matters . . .'

***

Mary understood Frank when he talked about time warp. It was Frank himself that had most of the confusion. 'I was only talking figuratively, Mary.'

'But Frank, what about the aerodrome that no longer exists?'

He frowned. 'You sure you didn't just sit down somewhere and, like . . .?'

'Like what, Frank? Dream it?'

'Well —'

'Did you dream the ancient cowherder? The way he moved? Dressed?'

Frank expelled pent up air. 'What about the drunk?' He digressed, animatedly, waving his grey hand. 'And there's the guy in the van. He didn't look real. Could've been in the movies. He said nothing, either. Yet he did! Thoughts. Waves of 'em. I dunno, Mary. I've heard of people dead tired who've had hallucinations. Perhaps . . .'

Mary wrung her hands. 'You think we both got hallucinations, Frank?' She watched his growing alarm with sadness. Frank was so used to being in control of things — equipment, crises — that his helplessness was spilling across the table from him with disruptive force.

'What about the drunk?' he repeated.

'You mentioned —'

'He said, "I want your life." That's how I feel, right now . . .'

Mary stared at him, his helplessness hurting her, making him a shadow of what he normally was: solid, real. 'We have life, Francis.'

'Do we?' He grasped her grey hand with his. 'The drunk frightened me so much, I nearly ran him over. I just jumped on the accelerator and drove straight at him.'

'Did he jump out of the way?'

Frank stared into his memory, mesmerised by its spell. 'I just lost sight of him. He was there, right there, as bold as brass, hammering on the windscreen in Mangle Street. Then he wasn't.'

Mary patted his hand. 'I think the figure in the van would have scared me the most.'

Frank laughed suddenly. 'Is it because he was like a biblical vision, Mary?'

Mary's eyes felt large in her head. 'Not just that, Francis . . .' From the periphery of her vision, she became aware of the silent Lucille. The girl had turned her head. The slight motion of the blonde halo was enough to remind Mary. Lucille wasn't grey like the surrounding air of New Casterleck. Like Tommy said, she had her own colour.

'It was what the man did.'

'Mary, he did and said nothing!'

'Thoughts. You felt his thoughts.'

'Yeah. He took over my mind, Mary. He paralysed me. Yet I didn't feel scared like I should have done. Thoughts . . . Massive, great flood of thoughts!'

'You said he put his right hand on your shoulder, then genuflected with his left. Is that right?'

'Yes, Mary!'

'What he did,' she murmured, 'was a technical blasphemy, Francis. You have to make the sign of the Holy Cross with your right hand . . .'

SEVEN

CACKLING laughter.

It sounded like the senile perversity of a tired old woman, growing in volume until it almost blocked Mary's ears.

She and Frank were still sitting at the table in their pebble-dash council house in New Casterleck. They should have been happy she felt, and giving thanks for the fresh start to their (earthly) lives. Instead, they were clinging to each other in the grey dreariness in the face of the derision of their own daughter.

Lucille's jaws looked impossibly wide beneath the alien curtain of straight, blonde hair. Only when the girl regained control of her capricious mirth were the gapped teeth finally covered.

'Are you telling me that crossing yourself with your left hand is a mortal sin?'

Mary swallowed away her dryness. 'I-I used the word "blasphemy" in the technical sense, Lucille. It's all in the Catechism.'

The whimsical laughter poured once more from the rosy features and the striking blonde halo. 'I've never mocked your beliefs, Mum. I just think you're carrying things too far for this day and age. Why was God sitting in the self-drive, anyway? Has his fiery chariot broken down, then?'

'Lucille!' Fear clutched at Mary's heart, letting only the single choked name through her frozen larynx.

The confident, strangely adult voice continued. 'I know, Mum: "Be ye not deceived, the Lord is not mocked. Whoever soweth the seed", and all that. We've all had these things shoved down our necks in this house.'

'For your own good, child! These are difficult times.'

Lucy shook her blonde mane. 'Most people nowadays couldn't even quote the bit I just did. I'm only trying to get you in touch. Maybe it's Darwin's Theory, the Swinging Sixties, Science. Blind Faith isn't it anymore . . .'

They sat in dread silence for a few seconds more.

'I wonder,' said Mary, 'if those things add up to the reason for all this . . .'

'All what, Mum? According to you, we've got till six o'clock by your watch to get out of Casterleck.' The blonde girl shook her head, smile twisting. 'Just think about it, Mum. Suppose I said I like Casterleck and want to stay put. Will the sky split open? What will happen, Mum?'

Frank cleared his throat. 'Take it easy, Lucy. You're mother's just . . .' His voice trailed away. The look Lucy shot him was malevolent, heightened into white horror by the colour.

Mary decided not to notice. 'As your mother, Lucille, I owe it to you and Thomas to look after you the best way I can. I don't presume to know what will happen if we stay here. Someone has told me it could be bad. I must try . . .'

Frank gave up trying to stare his daughter out. A shadow crossed his soul as he looked away. He clapped his hands together.

'OK,' he said. 'I have to take the van back, then return to sign on for five. We'll all go. What's barmy about that?'

'What for, Dad?'

'So that we can see what's out there!'

Lucy laughed again, Endlessly, it seemed. Mockingly.

'All right,' he went on hurriedly. 'Seeing is believing, right? Talk is never enough. If we start now, we can be back on the bus in good time if there's a change of mind.'

'Francis!' Mary was panicking again. 'What about Tommy?'

Conscious of Lucy's sly smile of triumph, Frank said. 'We'll look for him in the van. Now come on . . .'

***

'**What** ya wriggling around for, dude?' The shadow that was Rick just lay in the driver's seat of the old, black Capri like a sick man next to Tommy. Only his hands and feet moved. He'd pulled on black PVC gloves that creaked on the wheel like the joints of an old man.

Tommy sensed the aura of illness and disease. Even the smell of them wafted, faint, but persistent. Turning his head, the boy tried to penetrate the shadow of the glimpse of an eye or a tooth. The shade cast by the direct, overhead, private sun was too deep.

'I'm looking for the seat belt, Rick.'

There was a rumble of laughter as the house units fizzed by faster and faster.

'Earthly cares, man. Earthly cares . . .'

The beat language was dated. Even funny. The pursuit of plea-sure-for-its-own-sake antics of Rick seemed wild and perpetually juvenile. Stale.

The speed he sought with his clumping Chelsea boot was concrete.

Suddenly, the black gloves spun the wheel. The houses circled through a ninety degree arc as the tail came round. In seconds they were bouncing, jolting, down a single-track road that wound through the woods down an incline. Tommy gaped as he finally realised no seat belts were in fact fitted. And the speedo: 50, 60, 70.

'This is a bad road, Rick.'

The damaged voice wheezed its fatalistic dogma of a bygone era. 'The bad roads are the roads to ride. If you want a ride you get your wheels and you ride your ride to wherever and whatever, man . . .'

The sun. It had fallen back behind the windshield. Now it was swinging back as the gradient altered. The line of shadow crept inexorably up Rick's arms and chest, encased as they were in the stale, black leather. A black glove left the wheel and flipped open the glove compartment. The lid swung crazily above Tommy's jeans. Tapes and CDs poured over his lap like lice: Elvis, Cochrane, Holly, Joplin, Hendrix.

The glove emerged clutching a pair of old wraparound shades.

The open compartment released a further musty smell just as stale as the faintly rotting aroma already building.

The passing wood now climbed across the black, convex lenses as Rick donned the shades. And the line of shadow climbed on up his arms and chest. Funny. Where the biker's jacket parted were areas of white like bone. The sun, meanwhile, fell to the horizon

— right in front. Behind the swirling dust trail of the Capri, darkness and mist gathered, even stars in the sky. And the moon shone with the cratered features of an open mouthed man.

The last rays of the failing sun just touched the face of Rick.

Tommy's jaw fell in terror.

The eyeless sockets were hidden behind the wraparound shades, but the delineated cheekbones were open to the air. So were the naked teeth, grinning in perpetual rictus. The nose just wasn't there anymore, only the gaping nasal passageways that led right up into the rotting skull. The skull was joined to the upper vertebrae by crudely knotted wire.

Tommy's eyes popped.

Yellow things were falling down the leather front of Rick's jacket.

Maggots.

Tommy shrank in horror against the jerking passenger door. Just as the speedometer needle touched ninety, he was able to speak, or at least to squeak: a phrase, repeated over and over like a computer loop.

'Mum. Let me wake up, Mum. Mum. Let me wake —'

The jerking, maggot spilling skull turned to Tommy, pinned as he was against the car door and side window. Stale air flowed over the boy's frozen face as the wheeze emerged, real or imagined.

'I want your life.'

***

Mary watched Frank lock the door of their pretty, little house.

'Don't forget the mortise lock.'

Peels of laughter played from Lucy.

'That should keep out evil spirits, Mum!'

It was true that she felt foolish, standing there in her head scarf, making sure everything was locked up, as if things were as they'd always known them. Yet she didn't feel herself.

Mary Carter felt as grey and as wan as she knew she looked. Francis, too, didn't have the solidity she was used to. The mortise key was turning in the lock, the other keys meshing together, yet there was no jingle. There was no shadow in the cinders and mud at their feet. Just grey. A lack of light. The very air seemed to be unwilling to be sucked into their lungs, and the blood felt thin in the veins.

Not so Lucy, standing there in the mystery striped dress, hand on hip. Her very vitality seemed to laugh at her parents, as though their life forces were fading.

Mary glanced at her watch. Twelve o'clock.

'Tick, tock,' taunted Lucy.

'Don't mock, Lucille.' Mary fingered her crucifix. 'I'm trying to think.'

Francis put an arm about her shoulders. It felt cold. 'We can either wait for Tommy, or go and look for him.'

But Mary wasn't listening. Her head was lowered in silent prayer. She could tell her lips were moving because Lucy was sniggering.

Frank said, 'You could hang on here while I take a quick spin round the estate.'

Mary raised her head, opened her eyes, took a breath.

'Enjoy that?' sniggered Lucy.

'We must stick together,' said Mary. From her bag she took the memo pad she used for shopping, found her ball pen.

TOMMY — WAIT HERE TILL WE GET BACK IN A FEW MINUTES.

Automatically, she scribbled beneath: LOVE MUM.

Carefully, she trapped it in the letterbox flap.

'Francis, drive us all round the estate once. We'll come back here.'

***

The nightmare skull faded back into shadow as the sun dipped below the burning horizon. Rick discarded the shades and flicked on the heads. Bushes and couch grass lashed at the windscreen, etched white against the velvety dark grey of the night.

Night, thought Tommy.

Up the long hill they flew, leaving the woods and the moors behind, until they met the sky. A grey cloak of cloud closed around them. All sense of vibration had gone. It felt as though they were actually flying.

By now, Tommy Carter was clinging to the back of the seat.

'Mum! This isn't real! I promise I'll never ever never ever land in the shit ever again!'

Beside him, the wheezing croak splayed more rotting air. 'When you ride with Rick, everything's a dream, man . . .'

Tommy goggled through the windscreen. The light was increasing. There was a glow. Unholy. The cloud tore like silken fabric. A great plain of artificial light appeared as the last of the silk shredded away.

They were flying low over a great metropolis too futuristic ever to have been built. Not enough dosh. Every street and window was etched in artificial ice fire.

'Shit!' said Tommy.

'Right on!' wheezed Rick.

A terrible agoraphobia seized Tommy as the black car floated them over the vision of light and glass. As a vision, it was incredibly detailed. Fourteen year old council kid or not, Tommy automatically looked for practical, verifiable details, even without realising it.

The tops of the skyscrapers, for instance — they swept by ahead of their bases far below, thus obeying the laws of perspective. Computer simulation could do it, he felt. But as they lost height and sank to the level of the upper windows, Tommy saw that they were more than just painted in squares. There were people in there: sitting, standing, walking. Their clothes looked odd — sleek, functional, perfect.

The loops of the slip roads overlaid a lower grid pattern of ordinary roads lit by the comparatively dull sodium lighting he was used to. Down there, everything was slow and normal and boring, though no-one was on foot. Up on the flash flyovers, even the vehicles in the traffic streams looked unreal: too swish and toy-like. He could have been looking at a full-motion-video comic.

That was it!

It all looked too gaudy and mechanical — a hi-tech model. There was no sign of ordinary disorder, of human awkwardness, happiness, madness — just empty light and surface activity for the sake of activity.

'Balls!' cried Tommy.

The rotting skeleton turned to look. 'There are no balls with Rick!' Then it shoved a black gloved hand to mouth.

Tommy laughed till his wide eyes seeped tears. 'Proves it's not real! I'm getting out, man!'

'You can't get out, dude. Your life is mine.'

'Balls!'

Tommy decided he would open the door. He'd bail out like a paratrooper, wake up in his own bed where everything was real (well, sort of), explain his dream to Mum who would not understand it. The way of the world, yeah?

'Balls!'

He imagined himself doing it. Opening the door. Falling out.

The skull above the biker's jacket turned again to look. The lights that were now passing cast multi-shadows in the eye sockets and in the cavern of the perpetually grinning mouth as the jawbone opened in terror. Rick was dead. Tommy was certain, now. No question of betrayal. Skeletons didn't drive old Capris that had been smashed to shit in old RTAs six months previously, even if they were dressed in Rick's clothes and ring.

'Has to be a nightmare, right?'

Sure, people were moving inside the lit up oblongs of the floating windows, but they all just walked or sat or stood, like badly directed film extras. They performed robotic actions like computer sims. No-one argued, washed, watched TV, bonked or took a dump.

It wasn't real.

Tommy opened the front passenger door of the black Capri.

He could hear the rush of the airflow, feel it pressing the door against his muscles. He could taste the cold damp of the night, smell the megawatts of electricity and excitement, even hear the hum of the power currents and feel the way they made his skin throb.

But Tommy pushed the door wide — wide enough for it to hold on the hinge (that air should've pushed it shut, see?).

'Balls!'

He could see half a kilometre of convincing looking space beneath the angle formed by the sill and the door. The skull was convincing too. It looked across at Tommy, lower jaw dropping in fright, the vocal wheeze pouring its foul air into the slipstream as a single word reached Tommy's ears just before he launched himself into electric space.

'Please...'

***

Mary finally allowed Frank to pull away from their little house. They jolted over the rutted mud of the ring road, Lucille between them in front.

'Not too fast, Francis.'

Frank was changing up to third on the dual function gearbox, the steering wheel leaping beneath his hand. Lucy leant forward, the blonde hair swishing, the flesh coloured finger pointing.

'What's that in the road, Mum?'

Frank and Mary Carter peered at the road ahead. A column of air shimmered, bringing flecks of orange and gold to the pervading grey.

***

The skeleton in Rick's clothes watched the boy slip out of the passenger door of the Capri into the electrically charged night air.

The skeleton was flabbergasted. He'd never seen a mortal so disbelieving of the albeit primitive senses he relied upon. Aghast, the shape stared in horror through the windscreen, knowing all too well from his main right brain what was to come.

The Capri's headlights now lit up a country road that, despite its windings, was wide enough to allow two vehicles to pass. The Capri was in the act of taking the bend too fast, causing it to cut into the opposite carriageway. Light from oncoming heads was already burning into the hedgerows. There was the long wail of an air horn, the hiss of air brakes, the squeal of big, multi-axle tyres.

The articulated Tanker could not hold a straight course. Not enough road. The tail wobbled, swung round to sweep sideways down both carriageways, sidelights sparkling along its lengths like a glowing pier. The scythe action of the girder chassis swept low over the long bonnet of the skidding Capri. It decapitated everything that projected above the level of the bottom edge of the crumpling windscreen.

Triplex glass and flesh showered.

The dark head within popped up between car roof and lorry chassis. It powered away like a struck football, deep into the woods . . .

***

Lucy went right on pointing over her parents' shoulders.

Frank had seen thermals in summer that looked like this — but not the coloured flecks of light. Instinctively, he swerved to miss. A dark shape disappeared into the blind spot just behind and below the cab. It rolled in the mud. A bundle of rags?

He applied the brakes. A plume of dust rose in the offside mirror. Mary was already alighting from the nearside passenger door, followed by Lucy.

The dark bundle lay in the road. Frank felt his skin cool as blood drained from his face. At first there was no movement. Then the bundle stirred. Limbs took shape. They identified themselves as such in the messages passing from the rods and cones of Frank's retinae to his brain. Hands clawed in the mud. A tousled head lifted.

Mary took the bundle in her arms as Frank flew out of the cab. 'Tommy?'

The boy scrambled stiffly to his feet, his arms still round his mother. He looked wild, staring about him in disbelief.

'Hey! I'm alive!'

Frank grasped his son. He saw that the boy's hair was sticking out fan-wise, as if he'd been caught in a furious slipstream. His cheeks and knuckles were grazed, his coat sleeve torn.

'What have you been doing, Tommy?'

The boy's crazed look alighted on Lucy.

She was standing in her striped dress, blue eyes burning as if in unspoken warning.

'What has happened to your hair, Thomas?' Mary was fingering it with growing apprehension. Its colour had changed from mid-brown.

To b l a c k .

***

The station commander of RAF Casterleck sat behind his desk. Group Captain Gabriel's smile was thin and contemplative. He set aside the dossier on the Carter family carefully, and removed his horn beam spectacles. At length, he pressed the intercom.

'Anything new on the Carters?' The little man listened. Nodded. The monkey smile never slipped. 'Send in the sergeant of the guard.'

Moments later, he had to endure the foot stamping and the shamefaced report.

'I have reason to believe, sir, that they are leaving the estate in their own vehicle. Permission to send out patrols, sir.'

'At ease, Sergeant. Take a seat.'

'Sir!'

The sergeant pulled up the very chair used by Mrs Mary Carter during her interview not long before. The group captain smiled as broadly as ever, and slid across a tin of fifty Players Medium.

'Thank you, sir.'

Gabriel lit one himself and smiled on through the thin skeins of blue-grey smoke. 'Do you know that when we defeat the Hun, Sergeant, people will say that these things won the war?' He gestured with the cigarette.

'Even the bods at the bomb dump say that, sir.'

The groupie nodded. 'But when the status quo has been re-established and the threat to life and limb diminished, they will be used as a scapegoat for disease natural and manufactured, inexplicable fires not worth investigating properly, and social ills of all kinds.'

'Sir?'

'Changing opinion, that's all. We know, of course, that the real problems are rooted in human nature.'

'Sir!'

'Our work here is not just a question of scalp hunting and results, Sergeant. Take the Carter family. They aren't such a bad lot, comparatively speaking.'

The sergeant bared his teeth beneath the bar of his moustache. They had to pause while a Lanc took off for an air test, shaking the windows as its shadow flicked overhead. Soon, its four Merlins receded.

'Frank Carter, for instance. What do you think?'

The sergeant exuded disapproval from beneath his slashed peak. 'Just another damned civvy, sir!'

The groupie's smile broadened as he spread his hands. 'The war is about civilians, Sergeant. It's waged upon civilians, by civilians.'

'Sir! If you put it that way, sir, yes, sir!'

'Frank Carter is a humble bus driver. Did you know he was kind enough to give a lift to a chappie who scrambled out of last night's prang at nought feet? He was unaccounted for. Didn't know where he was!'

'So he should have, sir. With respect, sir!'

The groupie went on forcing himself to smile through his weariness. 'I bet you could quote the KRs to the last para, Sergeant.'

'Without Order there is Chaos, sir. That is my, er . . .'

'*Raison d'être?*'

'Sounds like it, sir.'

'Sir, sir, sir . . .'

'Sir?'

'There is the letter of the law, and the spirit of the law. Do you follow me, Sergeant?'

The regimental sergeant of the guard fidgeted in his seat. 'What about Thomas Carter, sir? The construction crew will not wear any palliative with regard to him, sir.'

Gabriel nodded heavily. 'Judging by the consequences of his actions, Sergeant, their emotional involvement is more than understandable. You realise, however, that duty forbids us the luxury of private vengeance. The boy is only fourteen. He is also officially classified as a Fool, as amended by the Milton Criterion. It's a question of his Malice Aforethought as balanced against his Responsibility for Action, Sergeant.'

The sergeant of the guard bristled. 'At fourteen, I was thrashed unmercifully for a fraction of this, sir!'

'I understand.'

'More than I do, sir. I had standards rammed down my throat with a buckled belt at home, the cat o' nine tails at school and the workhouse, and worse in the service, sir. Now it's this miserable lot's turn.'

Gabriel nodded sympathetically. 'It's the era we are born in that causes these confusions and frustrations, I fear. Comparison with one's contemporaries has to be the criteria.' The groupie leaned closer to his NCO. 'In the forest, when confronted with the dire consequences of his actions, the boy was genuinely contrite, Sergeant.'

The sergeant bared his teeth. 'Only because his prosecutor frightened seven colours of shit out of him, sir! With respect, sir!'

'Possibly,' smiled Gabriel wearily. 'Now I believe the construction crew victims are in pursuit. Is this true, Sergeant?'

The beginnings of near colour stung the NCO's cheeks, but quickly dissipated to the regulation Grey. 'Yes, sir!'

Smile returning in full force, the station commander settled back in his chair with his cigarette. 'Then we'll simply have to let matters resolve themselves, Sergeant . . .'

***

Tommy Carter seemed no worse for wear. When pressed (under Lucy's glare) he said, 'I, er, fell from the sky!'

Frank shook his head. 'It's as good a story as I've heard yet in this place,' he said. 'It'll have to do for now. Are you fit to travel?'

'Tommy is always ready to ride, man. Let's *motavate*!'

Aware of Lucy's smirk, Frank held the door back while they all climbed in, children in the middle. As Mary was helped up into her seat, she cocked her head.

'What's that noise?'

They could all hear it as they waited on the ring road: a high pitched buzz.

'That's a chain saw, dude,' said Tommy. 'Someone's getting it on sawing in the woods. Earthly cares, man. Earthly cares . . .'

Frank shrugged, climbed behind the wheel. 'Let's go.'

'Yo, dude!'

Frank choked. 'What videos have you been watching, Tommy?'

As Tommy and Lucy exchanged secret looks, Mary fingered her crucifix. 'We must find out what lies beyond the Grey.'

The Transit roared back into life. Frank let it pull away down the empty ring road. Dust plumed from the wheels and hung in the mist that was seeping back out of the silent trees . . .

As the self-drive droned eerily past the side track taken by the old, black Capri, the high pitched buzz ceased. There was the throb of a large engine starting up. Doors slammed.

Before the dust had settled from the passage of the van, a large, open back truck reared up from the side track. Heavy, ribbed tyres slapped down on the dried out mud of the ring road. Yellow hard-hats clustered and bobbed in the cab. They also weaved through the splits of the part wrecked site cabin lashed in the back.

From the cab fell a section of sawn tree trunk. it bounced end over end in the mud, ignored by the silent staring workmen.

From behind the wheel, the harsh, ruined features of White Hat glared with unremitting vengeance.

EIGHT

AS the self-drive Transit gathered speed, Mary peered out of the side window with sadness. The little pebble-dash house was well out of sight now. Much as council estates were sneered at by luckier, grander people than herself, Mary felt their new home had represented hope. Tommy could have met a different peer group and been less inclined to stray. Lucille might have outgrown her weakness. Mary was only too aware of it, her antennae tuned to every nuance of her daughter's deceptions and fantasies.

Perhaps that was it. Kids had fantasies and wanted to turn them into reality — real-life, waking dreams where nothing went wrong and no price was ever paid.

As for herself and Francis . . .

Mum and Dad. With less anxiety, they might have secured that sparkling togetherness that kept getting interrupted, put on Hold, postponed, until it faded with shelf life, like a cheap, overworked battery . . .

The sight of the still unoccupied houses windmilling past felt sad. Were they not blank units waiting to be filled in, enlivened, by a vibrant community of separate families who were making similar fresh starts?

Between the rows, Mary saw the square tower.

Was it real? What of the yellow hatted men who'd crowded its rail that morning?

Peering intently, Mary was able to make out movement still. A single figure emerged. She watched him stretch out a leather gauntlet to grasp the rail. She could see the paler grey of the sheepskin collar. The helmeted head travelled slowly, like a gun turret, following the path of her flight.

Hallucination?

She'd read somewhere that hallucinations symbolised something. Guilts. Fears. Sounded Freudian. Freud was supposed to be decried by modern psychologists. Was he false, or too honest?

Ten tenths cloud, Mary. One day you'll be old enough to see through the Grey in the world. You'll be guiding others through the flak . . .

Where had the words really come from? They just powered into her mind as the distant figure watched. The voice she recognised easily enough as Father's, but . . . A trick of memory, perhaps; a wish for guidance that was no longer there, winging its way across the years, a generation, foreshortening distances of time and space to render them meaningless. All with the power of thought . . .

As Mary fingered her crucifix, her lips moved.

***

The open back truck followed the wisp of dust that hung above the mud surface of the ring road. White Hat's orange cagoule crinkled as his gloved hands turned the wheel of the truck. His site boots tramped on clutch and accelerator — seldom the brakes.

The yellow hardhats that pressed about him moved as one, synchronised by single motion and purpose. The motion was Forward, the purpose, Death.

The right boot of White Hat pressed on the gas at every straight, gaining ground at every opportunity offered. The bobbing radiator grille strained ever forward like the bared canines of an indomitable predator.

Soon they could see the cause of the wisps of dust — the rear of the Transit peeping just before a fresh radius appeared along the ring road.

Beneath the yellow hardhats bobbed the angry faces.

Grey and white.

Like those of soldiers from Hell.

***

Frank Carter slowed at the junction that marked the exit off the New Casterleck estate. There was no traffic, so he was able to make the turn at the old fashioned Slow sign, and work his way back through the gears.

He felt a mixture of relief and regret as he allowed the Transit to pick up more speed down the long, straight hill through more woodland. In the distance he could see the spot where the Light had come. He pondered on what had really happened . . .

The light had grown in the grey mist until it had turned the windscreen into an impenetrable wall of luminosity. He could remember no impact. No trauma. They'd entered the wall of luminous air. Then they'd arrived at their new home.

What had happened in between remained a blank . . .

Consequently, Frank Carter could not help but slow as they neared the spot. As if a signal had been given, Mary Carter ceased praying and stared through the windscreen. Frank could see her frowning.

Perhaps she was still in her reverie. She said. 'Gateway . . .'

'What's that, Mary?'

'It was a gateway, Francis, from one world to the next . . .'

Between them, the strange black hair of Tommy began to vibrate. The boy was spluttering with mirth. Whimsical laughter. His eyes shone with it. Wildly. His cheeks. They'd lost their teenage puppy fat. It was a hard cynical face that laughed. Harsh. Derisive.

Now the boy began to hum a series of mocking notes. The theme from *Close Encounters*? No. They'd been repeating a cult series on the Box from years ago. *The Twilight Zone*.

From the mouths of babes and sucklings, thought Frank.

Lucy joined in. '"Be ye not deceived. The Lord is not mocked. For whoever soweth the seed, so shall he reap the whirlwind." Ha-ha-ha. Jim, lad!'

'Lucille . . .' Mary sounded sad.

'Mother . . .' Lucy parodied.

Whirlwind.

Was it a trick? A coincidence? From the word "whirlwind", Frank had another what-is-wrong-with-this-picture? feeling. Carefully, he surveyed the slowly passing frozen pictures of rural, lonely road with overhanging foliage. In seconds, he saw the difference.

Motion.

The picture was no longer Frozen in its endless shades of Grey. The overhanging boughs were now moving. Leaves trickled across the road like fleeing figures. Entire trees bent till they groaned before the weight of the natural element of air. Wind. Their branches looked like the desperately waving arms and entreating faces of the trapped inhabitants of the Grey that the Carters themselves were trying to escape.

The Grey itself was breaking up too. A curtain of flecked light was steadily drawing itself across the granite chips of the road surface — shimmering air that cascaded flecks of orange and gold.

'Gateway,' murmured Mary, as though still entranced.

There was sound too. A high pitched engine note caught Frank's ear, dragging his attention to the offside wing mirror.

Through the moving skeins of grey mist behind them he could make out the dancing headlights of a rapidly approaching heavy vehicle. It was moving far too fast for the prevailing conditions. Frank saw the entire chassis of the open back truck lift into the air as its driver paid no heed to the rolling undulations over which it passed.

Something else . . .

Flecks of yellow nodded over the side gates of the back of the truck.

Men.

Workmen in yellow hardhats were hanging on like grim death to a disintegrating structure lashed to the back of the madly speeding, bouncing truck. A piece of it sailed away in the blur like the broken wing of an aircraft. It twisted end over end in the building gale that was now tearing the grey mist to shreds.

'The mad bastards!'

Frank ducked his head as Mary leant behind him to stare through the offside mirror in dread.

Ahead, the curtain of shimmering light continued to draw inexorably across the road. Already it had sealed off their side of the carriageway. Now it was eating up the other side.

'Beat it,' said Mary, tonelessly. 'Beat it, beat it. Beat the light!' She checked her watch. 5.58pm!

Tramping the gas, monkey climbing the wheel, Frank made the van lurch forward and swerve round the far edge of the encroaching light . . .

Beyond it was the Grey.

Here, the mist was thicker than ever, untouched by the oddly localised freak wind. It hung in ever thicker shrouds across the undulating surface of the road. As they entered it, the road disappeared from sight. Frank grunted with effort as he straightened the van up, at the same time flicking on the heads and wipers.

Beads of moisture clung to safety glass and eyelashes. Breath steamed. The wipers squeaked like nemesis metronomes counting remaining seconds.

Frank flicked the switch on the top of the gear selector and dipped the clutch. The engine note smoothed as the gears climbed to the higher ratio. The speedo surged madly beyond sixty. The head beams just bounced back at them from a solid wall of flowing grey that seemed too lazy to part to let them through.

Darting his gaze to the offside mirror, Frank was in time to see the two glaring eyes of the truck lurch sickeningly round the edge of the curtain of flickering gold. The yellow hardhats swung like flower heads over the top of the cab as the truck teetered dangerously on its offside wheels like a Canadian stunt team vehicle.

Another flat piece of structure flew away into the trees whose branches lashed the tilted cab. Behind the wheel, the pale blob of the driver's hardhat remained disquietingly steadfast as he wrestled the centrifugal force.

The truck slammed back onto all wheels with an audible crash. A couple of swerves and squeals from the tyres, and the truck wobbled back into relentless pursuit mode.

The burning beams of the heads raced closer in the wing mirror.

'Hold tight!' Frank maintained pressure on the gas.

'What's happening?' asked Lucy, yawning.

All four of their heads jerked as one.

A shuddering impact struck the rear of the Transit. One of the rear doors bevelled inwards. It began waving in the slipstream. Tortured metal screamed. The two scorching eyes of the truck leered at them through the ripped gloom of the van interior.

Tommy laughed, black hair flicking. 'Bang goes your deposit, dude!'

Frank could not resist growling, 'Our deposit, smart ass! My wage goes into the household — your gut!'

'Earthly cares, man . . .'

Through the interior mirror, Frank caught a fleeting glimpse of the snarling front of the truck. One blazing headlight glared beyond the shearing door. That and the white hardhat and bared teeth of the maniacal driver bore down through the shredding mist.

Another bone jarring impact tore the door off altogether. It disappeared onto the fizz of the tearing road, crunching in an instant beneath the voracious maw of the wildly driven rig . . .

It took time, but the superiority of the powerful Transit engine with its dual function gearbox wrought space between the two vehicles — hunter and hunted.

With the needle hovering insanely on ninety, Frank listened to the singing note of the engine, hoping the oil level had been maintained. The oblong of the open door vibrated in the central interior mirror.

There were the transitory images of White Hat, his uncompromising grimace, glinting teeth projecting a constant stream of violent invective with all sound drowned, making them all the more malevolent. The pale blobs of the faces beneath the yellow hard-hats were robotic: simply programmed to automatically wreak vengeance, like cybernetic drones.

Some instinct caused Frank Carter to sneak a glance at Tommy.

The boy was craning his neck to stare in fascination through the oblong left by the torn off rear door. His excitement and curiosity seemed divorced from the real eventualities of what could happen if the jolting, madly driven rig made up the hard won ground now growing between the two vehicles.

'You're takin' 'em, dude! The driver's really uptight!'

And the black haired boy made a sophisticated single fingered gesture he wasn't supposed to know about — though all fourteen year olds Frank knew did, he thought ruefully.

'Don't wind 'em up anymore, son.'

As though the words were audible in the howling storm of the slipstream, the snarling front of the truck suddenly squeezed out the distance between. A blazing headlight reared almost inside the van interior.

White Hat's bared teeth were clearly seen before the curtain of flickering light suddenly drew . . .

***

'**Why** ya slowing down, man?'

Floating in blackness.

Tommy's voice came through quite clearly, but nothing else.

All vibration had gone. They felt they were floating in a Stygian void unconnected with road, or even Earth itself. Pressing accelerator, clutch or brake made no difference.

From across the space of the cab Mary's whispered prayer carried. 'Dear Saint Jude. Please pray for those of us who have recourse to thee . . .'

There was another whisper — air round the outer surfaces of the van.

Frank Carter checked all his mirrors, feeling cold and agoraphobic. Now that his eyes were becoming accustomed to near darkness, odd specks and skeins of light were visible — stars that did not twinkle, the glaring eyes of the pursuing rig's headlights.

Beyond these was something else: a luminous curtain; an actual edge to a reality of sorts. Though it was already receding, Frank could just make out miniature trees blowing in the now faraway gale.

He quickly snapped on the lights. This action made the panel glow green, elements of which reflected in the windows and screen, confusing the picture of their new surroundings.

Frank could still see Mary's bent head; still hear her whispered prayer. 'Dear Saint Jude . . .'

Most of all was the impression of falling between worlds, as though rejected by all. The distant road was now barely a glimmer, continually diminishing upward, the wavering fronds of its actuality increasing the impression of falling an unimaginable distance — though the other whisper, the slipstream, did not increase at all.

They might have been in a small aircraft locked into a descent path. As if to confirm this, Frank could make out a different light pattern ahead and below.

Suddenly, what looked like a firework crackled loudly. It left a jagged plume of white smoke. The pyrotechnic lit up half a church steeple which drifted far beneath them, briefly casting a spear-like shadow. Other fires were soft, stretched, red blobs, furry like glow worms. A great, mauve flash showed a glimpse of a power line writhing in tiny, dancing, brilliant, white sparks.

There was a voice — a very old radio voice, scarred by static. 'Plate Rack. Plate Rack. Come in to bomb.' Faint, as if only imagined . . .

Then Frank saw something moving. Then something else. Aircraft. Dozens of them. All were four engined, prop driven dinosaurs who made the air throb. They were descending through them. Whatever was below was coming up quickly. Every street in one area was etched in fire — over there to the left. Directly below, roads were just discernible, painted in red and orange by the raging fires. Frank could see tall, but old, buildings, as yet untouched. In the roads themselves were the tails of sparks.

A voice in his head made him flinch. He just knew it was from the Past . . .

See those little trails of sparks? That tells you when you surprise the Hun. The sparks are from street trams as they cross junctions — their wires short, see? When they know we're coming, they stop the trams.

Feel sorry for the Hun? Every man and woman below is dedicated to our destruction. If they're not bearing arms, they're working in the factories, making instruments to attend to our destruction. Kill or be killed — that's the choice when you are caught in the machine of War . . .

'No!'

The resounding negative had been Frank's own voice. Now another one was in his head. More authoritative.

. . . one of those terrible things that happens in wartime, brought about by an unfortunate combination of circumstances . . .

Now there was a document, stark on the screen of his consciousness. It was in German, but he could translate it:

Up to the evening of 20th March, 1945, 202,040 bodies, primarily of women and children, were recovered . . . Of the dead only some thirty percent could be identified . . . As the removal of the corpses could not be undertaken quickly enough, 68,650 of the bodies were incinerated, and their ashes interred on a cemetery. As the rumours far exceed reality, open use can be made of the actual figures.

p.p. The Commander of the Civil Police Chief of Staff
(Signed)
GROSSE
Colonel in the Civil Police
Dresden
22nd March, 1945.

'What is it?' gasped Frank. He'd spoken aloud. Mary's hand was laid lightly upon his own.

Her voice was calm. 'It's no-one's fault . . .'

The streets, old, foreign, strange, were rushing up quickly to meet them. They were passing below the level of the roofs. The trams had stopped. People were hurrying out of them, looking up at the night sky.

'I've seen sommat like this!' cried Tommy. 'We gotta get out!'

'No,' said Mary. 'Have faith . . .'

'What?'

Rushing up to meet them, the old German street was suddenly consumed by an ancient catastrophe whose true details had lain buried by history. The building firestorm linked across the previously untouched suburban area. Hair, clothes, buildings, trams, crowds, horses: all spontaneously ignited. A man-made wind of biblical proportions swept in. It uprooted trees, animals, running figures. Everything light and combustible was sucked upward in the vortex to a height of over 14,000 feet. Council documents would be found up to a hundred miles away.

All of the unfolding horror raced up to meet the Carter family.

***

Frank Carter's eyes were wide with concentration. He ducked his head.

The road poured on ahead of them. Half a mile distant was the T junction with the A road that led to civilisation.

As the speedo still climbed beyond ninety, the hazard drifted toward them at a frightening rate. Frank, lifting his right foot, peered closely at the intersecting highway for signs of traffic.

There were none. Just featureless Grey.

Their heads jerked again as the pursuing truck impacted.

The grinding collision crumpled the other rear door. Cracks of grey light appeared in it like a growing spider's web. The bolt snapped and the door flapped with increasing clatter.

Frank Carter weighed all the factors: speed falling below seventy, the chasing rig weaving to the offside, burning smell from the rear brake drums, shrieking rubber from the tyres — and still no sign of traffic on the rapidly closing main drag.

'They're gonna overtake, dude!'

The black haired boy still hadn't connected the adrenalin trip with the consequences to those he loved and who loved him.

'This isn't a video movie!' roared Frank.

Mary sat in calm serenity.

OK, but it was he who had to get them out of it. One day — maybe even right now — there'd be a computer simulation that could figure what to do next faster and surer. Right now, it was Frank Carter.

Continental drift.

It was an old fashioned term, Frank knew. Tommy would call it a tailspin. Not strictly true.

Frank's memory had thrown up an ancient racing picture. Stirling Moss. He was in the lead at a famous bend in an old motor race. The aerial photo showed Moss' car to be the only one at an angled attitude to the bend. Not a tailspin — a four wheel Continental Drift.

The old theory seemed to hold good. In a super-fast version of what a bus did on a test skid pan, the Transit shed rubber from all four wheels as it angled into the turn, the line of which took it across to the opposite carriageway of the adjoining A road.

The deep kerb on the far side drew close in a blur of speed. Even the kiss of a tyre wall would cause a blowout and upset the balance of the controlled dry skid of forward momentum against the sideways tug of centrifugal force.

Through the wing mirror, Frank caught the truck careering away. Its tail came round in unstoppable catastrophe that grew from loss of control.

White Hat roared out of the cab in defiance.

Because he knew.

The truck was now sliding backwards. The entire vehicle leapt over the deep kerb and footpath, through the old wooden fence into the mist laden meadow beyond. All in a millisecond.

As an afterthought, a yellow hatted figure flew like a discarded, child's doll in its wake.

Then it was gone . . .

Time: 6.00pm.

***

Colour. Noise.

They exploded into the midst of it. Instantly, they were surrounded by the life they thought they'd left behind. Headlights flared. Yellow hazards flashed. Light blazed all around as vehicles careened and swerved. A thirty-four ton juggernaut bore down on them, large and formidably there, swinging to its own nearside, cutting up a stream of frightened drivers in saloon cars who bunched and squeezed nose to tail and honked their horns in sterile protest.

Frank Carter yanked the wheel of the Transit.

Brought the van back to their own carriageway.

Horns still brayed. The driver of the juggernaut was yelling the usual obscenities, virtually hanging out of his cab. Cars began to pass, furious faces of road rage turning toward them.

Frank gasped heavily, laughed hysterically. Life!

Mary clung to his arm the moment he'd got the self-drive back under control. As the blare of horns and the glare of lights abated, Frank blinked at the green of the fields, the blue of the sky.

Through the windscreen, a platinum sun blazed directly on their faces.

Frank Carter gaped through the interior mirror into the gloom of the van interior. It was packed with furniture. Both rear doors were bolted securely in place, undamaged . . .

Beside him, Lucille tossed her brown curls. 'When are we going to get there, Dad?'

He gazed at his daughter. Her eyes had lost their wild burning, peeping sly through the curls instead. The gap toothed girlie smile was back. 'I'm hungry!' she said.

Tommy's mousy hair bobbed next to her as he stared in fascination at the traffic. 'Slow down, Dad. I think the turning's coming up . . .'

Frank's gaze shot to the sky. The sun. It was behind them. He could see their shadow, half on the road, half on the back of the car in front. He shook his head. The fact that they were now coming, instead of going to New Casterleck, and on a different day, was already becoming increasingly vague in his already fading memory.

By the time he noticed that Mary's lips were moving, and that tears were streaming down his face, all the trauma had gone, as if it had never been.

With some irritation, he snapped, 'Why are you crying, Mary?'

***

Outside the pebble-dash house unit, Frank lifted down the last of the furniture. Feeling warm in the sun, he stretched in the T shirt and took in a deep draught of country air. Then he looked across the rooftops towards the centre of the New Casterleck estate.

Slates shimmered in the slight heat haze. In the blue vault of the sky were the type of fluffy white clouds associated with dry, sunny weather. From the woods across the road came the hum of bees, the cheep of sparrows. High above, a lark twittered.

An electric whine turned his head. A milk float was humming round the corner on the freshly laid tarmac of the ring road. A pleasantly plump old man alighted from the float. 'I thought perhaps you folk would like a milk delivery.'

As Mary trotted down gratefully to give him her order, Frank was reminded of children's TV: Trumpton. This nudged a recent memory, but for the life of him he could not think what it was.

By the time Mary had carried across their first bottles of milk for their new home, an open back construction truck roared to a halt outside the pretty little house. It seemed dark, threatening. It was followed by a Range Rover.

Frank shook his head, puzzled by a feeling of *déjà vu*.

A man in a suit and a white hardhat got out of the Range Rover. 'We believe you people are our first residents. We hope you enjoy your stay.' He handed Mary a business card, which she carefully and deferentially put away in her handbag. 'Ring us at that number if you have any problems.'

One of the construction gang jumped down from the truck. A young man. He swaggered up to Lucille, who was slyly agog. 'What do you do of an evening?' he asked.

Lucy, aware of her mother's warning glance, hung her head. 'I dunno.'

'Do you . . . like . . . go out with boys?'

Frank hid behind his hand. Much amusement was also emanating from the other workmen hanging out the site cabin lashed to the back of the truck.

'Sometimes I do. Sometimes I don't,' said Lucy. 'OK?'

The young man in the yellow hardhat never ceased grinning. 'Fair enough. If I call tonight after work, will you be in?'

'I might be. On the other hand, I might not.'

'Is, er, that a Yes?'

'Maybe. Maybe not.'

'Er . . . Fair enough.'

To much barracking from the men in the front and rear of the truck, the young man walked back, climbed over the tailboard.

Again, Frank shook his head, enjoying the warm air and the clear light. He looked round for Tommy.

The boy was looking up at the cab of the truck.

The stone face of White Hat looked down.

'All right, son?' asked the foreman gruffly. 'You an apprentice tearaway?' His question was accompanied by a joint explosion of mirth from the yellow hats crammed in the cab.

'That's a big truck, Mister.' said Tommy.

'All the better to chase kids with.'

'What do ya do when you've caught 'em, Mister?'

'Eat 'em!'

More laughter. But only from the men in the yellow hats. White Hat resolutely showed no sign of jocularity, even when a mud caked hand stretched to dislodge his hardhat — his badge of authority.

Tommy gazed up from the brightness of the newly laid road. He squinted. 'What kind of brakes does your truck have?'

White Hat explained with a surprising patience

The boy smiled . . .

ALSO FROM TANJEN

THE PARASITE

Neal L. Asher

Jack is the pilot of a cometary miner. On his final mission, the one which will make him rich, he encounters something in the hold of his ship, something which has been held in the ice of a comet for millennia.

Set in the future of military take overs, rising sea levels, and satellite industries, this is a story of high tech subterfuge and violence, which asks; what is it to be human? And what might the human race become?

ISBN 0952718316 — Price £5.99

"top quality SF from one of genre's hotshot new talents"
Dragon's Breath

"anyone who cares about the future of British literary SF should check it out"
SFX

EYELIDIAD

Rhys H. Hughes

Baron Darktree is a highwayman searching for gold he buried when he was younger. It's bad enough he has to put up with insults from his younger self (now a portrait he carries on his back), and that the map tattooed on his eyelid is no longer visible, but when he gets mistaken for Beer'or, the pagan god of golden beer, he begins to wonder how bad things can get.
Oh, much worse . . .

ISBN 0952718324 — Price £5.99

"Richly and hilariously imaginative, teeming with memorable images, and inimitably Welsh"
Ramsey Campbell

"the jaded fantasy reader will find much to enjoy here"
Flickers 'n' Frames

"imaginative slice of surrealist fantasy"
Samhain

RECLUSE

Derek M. Fox

A letter from a mysterious woman is all it takes to turn
Daniel Lees's world upside-down. He suspects his wife of having an affair. He believes his children are in danger from
something that stalks the moors. He is haunted by a past that
will not leave him alone.
Finally he has to face up to what he really is and battle against
the nightmare that has threatened to destroy everything he
holds dear.

ISBN 1901530000 — Price £5.99

"*Recluse* is the chilling journey into the heart of a nightmare.
Reader beware – Derek M. Fox is set to be a new Master of Fear."
Mark Chadbourn

"maintaining a cracking pace and an iron grip on the reader's
attention."
BBR Directory

MESMER

Tim Lebbon

When Rick sees his ex-girlfriend at a motorway service station he knows he must be losing his mind. For Penny had been brutally murdered and left to rot in a ditch eight years earlier. In trying to find answers to insane questions Rick finds himself immersed in a world where the dead can live again, a world controlled by the evil powers of the Mesmer.

ISBN 1901530027 — Price £5.99

"Mesmer is absolutely superb. Lebbon's going to be big one day. Start reading him now."
Simon Clark

SCATTERED REMAINS

Paul Pinn

A collection of short stories to celebrate the 750th anniversary of the Bethlem Mental Hospital, the origin of the word bedlam. Each story is an examination of mental illness within the dark underbelly of human nature. Make sure you read this with the lights on.

ISBN 1901530051 — Price £6.99

"Soul-searing . . . totally bleak, remorseless and nihilistic."
Pam Creais, Dementia 13

"I swooned at the power, the vividness of the imagery."
Andy Cox, The Third Alternative

"Bleak, claustrophobic, full of dirt and death . . . I like it."
Dave Logan, Grotesque Magazine

SCAREMONGERS

It will take a brave man or woman to read through this collection in one sitting. Each story needs a deep breath before starting and a moment of reflection on completion. All your fears are here and if you remain umoved by the end – you must already be *dead*.
Not for the fant-hearted.

A collection of short stories from some of the big names in horror — Ramsey Campbell, Ray Bradbury, Michael Marshall Smith, Simon Clark, Mark Chadbourn, Stephen Laws, Poppy Z. Brite, Stephen Gallagher, Dennis Etchison, Freda Warrington, Steve Harris, Ben Leech, Peter Crowther, Nicholas Royle and many more.
All royalties donated to Animal Welfare Charities

ISBN 1901530078 — Price £6.99

COMING IN 1998

DEMON

Derek M. Fox

Tibb's Cove ought to be a pleasant seaside town. But when a Lancaster Bomber drops out of the night sky, and out of the past, shooting up the place, it's anything but.

It's all to do with the war, and the game a group of local boys played on the old airfield in 1954.

What dark secrets do the townspeople keep hidden? And why is the aircrew back to terrorise the skies, exacting their terrible revenge?

A cracking follow-up to *Recluse*.

ISBN 1901530019 — Price £5.99

THE HOMEMAKERS' WITCHES COVEN

Michael F. Korn

Keith has managed to infiltrate the local witches coven, who as far as he can see are just a bunch of old hags who spend most of their time shopping at malls and gossiping about their neighbours. But as he digs deeper he begins to suspect there is more here than he originally thought. The question is: how deep does he go?

A wicked satire that scratches away at the benign surface of small town America, opening up an underbelly of naked ambition, sexual perversion and deals with the Devil.

ISBN 1901530035 — Price £5.99

All TANJEN titles are available from good bookshops or can be ordered direct (post and packing free)

The Parasite — £5.99..Neal L. Asher

Eyelidid — £5.99..Rhys H. Hughes

Prisoners of Limbo — £5.99..David Ratcliffe

Mesmer — £5.99..Tim Lebbon

Scattered Remains — £6.99..Paul Pinn

Scaremongers — £6.99..Various

Cheques/POs made payable to Tanjen Ltd

Name:...

Address:..

....

....

send orders to: Tanjen Ltd, 52 Denman Lane, Huncote, Leicester, LE9 3BS

THE VERY BEST OF BRITISH . . .

Discover the bright new face of publishing in the British small press.

From established, award-winning magazines to brand new titles brimming with attitude, you'll find every kind of SF, fantasy and horror, plus some you've never dreamed of.

Now this thriving scene is brought together for you to explore in a brand new catalogue from the New SF Alliance.

Whether you're a writer researching new markets, or a reader fed up with banal high street fiction, there's something to suit every taste.

And not only is the NSFA Catalogue the quickest, simplest and most convenient way to sample this exciting market, but it doesn't cost you a penny.

For a copy of our free catalogue, send a large SAE to NSFA, c/o Chris Reed, PO Box 625, Sheffield S1 3GY, UK, or visit <http://www.syspace.co.uk/bbr/nsfa-cat.html>.

With 7 issues under its belt Night Dreams continues to deliver a
magazine that delves into the gruesome world of fiction by some of
the best talents around.

From stories, poems & strange but true paranormal experiences
Night Dreams is a quarterly A4 publication with approximately 15
stories per issue

Single issue - £2.80   Four issue subscription - £10.50

Please make cheques/POs payable to Kirk S. King
send to: Night Dreams, 47 Stephens Road, Walmley,
Sutton Coldfield, W. Midlands, B76 2TS